"You need to let them know about your condition."

Startled, Lauren declared, "No way. The fewer people who know, the better."

"It's nothing to be ashamed about."

"You don't understand. People look at you differently when they're aware of weird medical conditions." Poor, pitiful Lauren wasn't the way she wanted to live. "I don't want anyone feeling sorry for me. Particularly the people who work here. I have an image to uphold."

Jake stared at her. She wanted to turn away but couldn't.

"You're too proud to accept that someone might care you have this condition that forces you to hide yourself away from life?"

TERRY FOWLER is a native Tarheel who loves calling coastal North Carolina home. Single, she works full-time and is active in her small church. Her greatest pleasure comes from the way God has used her writing to share His message. Her hobbies include gardening, crafts, and genealogical research. Terry invites everyone to visit her web page at terryfowler.net.

Books by Terry Fowler

HEARTSONG PRESENTS

HP298—A Sense of Belonging
HP346—Double Take
HP470—Carolina Pride
HP537—Close Enough to Perfect
HP629—Look to the Heart
HP722—Christmas Mommy
HP750—Except for Grace
HP793—Coming Home
HP841—Val's Prayer
HP862—Heath's Choice
HP878—Opie's Challenge
HP942—Peace, Be Still
HP962—With Not a Spoken Word

Just One Touch

Terry Fowler

Heartsong Presents

To those who suffer with sleep disorders. Thanks RealCutie for your input. To our heavenly Father—thank you for the opportunity to write for your glory. To Heartsong Presents— thanks for allowing me to see my work in print.

A note from the Author:
I love to hear from my readers! You may correspond with me by writing:

Terry Fowler
Author Relations
PO Box 721
Uhrichsville, OH 44683

ISBN 978-1-61626-575-5

JUST ONE TOUCH

All scripture quotations are taken from the King James Version of the Bible.

This book is a work of fiction. Names, characters, places, and incidents are either products of the author's imagination or used fictitiously.

Our mission is to publish and distribute inspirational products offering exceptional value and biblical encouragement to the masses.

PRINTED IN THE U.S.A.

one

Surely she wasn't sleeping.

Jacob Greer could not believe his eyes when he stepped into the office of the chief financial officer and found Lauren Kingsley asleep in her chair. Obviously deep sleep since she did not respond to his throat clearing and other efforts to make her aware of his presence. No wonder Sleep Dreams needed a management consultant.

Ashleigh Fields, Lauren Kingsley's administrative assistant, entered the office carrying a salad and bottle of water. "Mr. Gre—Greer," she stuttered, looking horrified. "I'm sorry, sir, but you shouldn't be in here."

Obviously Sleeping Beauty didn't object to his presence. He eyed the young assistant, noting her extreme discomfort. "I plan to stay until Ms. Kingsley wakes."

"But, sir. . ."

"Go back to your desk, Ms. Fields. I'll deal with this."

"But you don't understand."

From the way she wailed the words, Jake thought maybe she feared losing her job. He took her arm and urged her out the door. "I appreciate your loyalty, but this type of behavior is precisely why I'm here."

She gasped and covered her mouth. "Oh sir, no. It's not what you think. I've never known anyone to work harder than Lauren."

Obviously she admired her supervisor. Perhaps Ms. Fields aspired to one day nap anytime she wanted as well. His brow wrinkled with the contemptuous thought, and the administrative assistant scurried from the room without another word.

5

Jake turned back to the slumbering woman. He'd never witnessed such flagrant abuse of a position. Prepared to wait her out, he took the seat facing the desk, leaned back, and crossed one leg over the other.

He would be the first person Lauren Kingsley saw when she woke. Then she would hear exactly what he thought of her sleeping on the job. Her father had hired him to help turn things around here at Sleep Dreams and that was what he planned to do.

Jake allowed his eyes to drift over her serene expression, feeling a stirring of appreciation. He couldn't see the color of her eyes, but long black eyelashes brushed her cheeks. Her long golden brown hair was parted down the center and lay about her shoulders. Her skin was a flawless ivory that rivaled that of a baby. She even slept like a newborn, he thought. But she needed to pay less attention to her social life and more to her job.

After several minutes, Jake glanced at his watch and back at the woman behind the desk. Suddenly it occurred to him something wasn't right here. Was she sick? Unconscious? It was ridiculous that she'd still be sleeping.

Greg Kingsley rushed into the room. "Jake, I'm sorry. I meant to tell you. . ."

Lauren's eyes fluttered open. Jake noted her surprise as she took in the two men in her office. "Daddy? Is something. . ."

"Everything's okay, honey," her father comforted, hurrying to her side. He patted her shoulder gently.

"No, it's not." Jake's earlier concern evaporated. She might be the Kingsleys' daughter, but she owed her parents for giving her this key position in their company. "What kind of example is she setting by sleeping on the job? I've been in this room for"—he paused and studied his watch for effect before he said—"ten minutes and she didn't know I was here."

Greg's voice grew stern as he said, "Now wait a minute. . ."

"No," Jake interrupted. "No more excuses. There's no room at Sleep Dreams for anyone who doesn't carry their share of the load."

Lauren's face turned pink. She should be embarrassed, Jake thought. But he saw something else. Surely she wasn't pretending to be hurt.

A sad smile curved her lips. "It's okay, Daddy. Go back to your office. I'll explain."

Greg Kingsley appeared highly agitated, his ruddy complexion growing redder by the minute. "I should have filled him in before now."

She touched his arm and pleaded, "Go back to work. Please, Daddy. Let me deal with Mr. Greer."

Deal? Jake stared at her. Did she think they were going to negotiate her right to sleep on the job?

Greg Kingsley kissed her forehead. "I'm sorry, Laurie."

Even though he didn't want to, Jake experienced that same rush of fatherly affection he felt for his own child. These two loved each other.

"It's not your fault. It's not anyone's fault. It just is." She squeezed his arm. "We'll talk later."

After he'd gone, she looked Jake straight in the eye and said, "It can't be helped."

"Sure it can. A little less social life and more rest at night and you won't require naps to get you through the day."

"I do hope all your decisions aren't based on snap judgments." Her soft tone admonished as her hazel eyes pinned him in place. "And for the record, my nap had nothing to do with late hours."

His brows lifted, questioning her comment. "Looked that way to me."

She shrugged. "I can understand your assumption, but things are not always as they seem."

Jake leaned back in the chair and waved his hand imperiously. "By all means, share your reasons for disrespecting your parents and abusing their trust in you."

He couldn't abide the spoiled rich kids who took their positions with family businesses for granted. Lauren Kingsley was in her mid to late twenties. She knew her father would never fire her. He'd strain the company budget further to hire someone to do her job. And in typical fashion of a spoiled brat, she'd take advantage of that knowledge.

"The situation happens to be. . ."

Both heads turned as Greg Kingsley burst into the room. "She can't help it. She's sick."

"Daddy! I said I'd handle this."

Jake saw frustration in her expression and heard exasperation in her tone.

Greg Kingsley's gaze focused on his daughter. "I won't have anyone criticizing you because of your problem."

Jake knew this man would fight the world to defend his child. He looked from one to the other. What did he mean by sick? She didn't look sick to him. A little tired maybe but if she was sick, why hadn't she stayed home to recuperate? Why bring her germs to the office to potentially risk infecting others? "You shouldn't come to work sick."

She smiled at that. "Don't worry. It's not contagious. I have narcolepsy. I'm sure you understand that it's not something we discuss openly. In fact, very few people within the company are aware of my disorder. My assistant generally keeps everyone out when I have an attack. She must have been away from her desk. The attacks often occur rather quickly."

"Bu–but. . ." Jake found himself stuttering this time.

"I won't have you berating her," Greg Kingsley emphasized, pinning him with his glare. "Lauren works rings around everyone in this company. No one works as many hours as she does."

Lauren rose and stepped around the desk. Jake took a moment to appreciate her long curly hair and curvy figure before giving her his full attention.

"It's okay, Daddy," she said softly, taking his arm and urging him toward her chair. "Perhaps we should explain and let Mr. Greer draw his own conclusions."

She chuckled and the hazel eyes brightened. "You have to admit that after watching me sleep for more than ten minutes he's entitled to feel I take advantage of your love for me." Lauren glanced at Jake and asked, "Don't you find it ironic that Sleep Dreams manufactures one of the most comfortable sleep systems in the world and the owner's daughter suffers from a sleep disorder?"

"I didn't realize," Jake choked out finally.

"It's okay," she offered, looking almost sympathetic. "I live with my problem. I hope you can do the same."

❧

Lauren wanted to sink through the floor. She'd asked her father to let her handle this, but in his usual overprotective manner, he'd raced to her rescue. Lauren had debated the situation for days, trying to determine the best plan of action. Her preference would have been to gradually ease into the truth with Jacob Greer. But today's incident had pretty much destroyed any possibility of that happening. Now they both dealt with the emotional fallout.

"I'm so sorry," he said for the fourth time since her father finally left. "I should have learned all the facts before jumping to conclusions."

"It's not a problem, Mr. Greer."

"Jake, please."

"I'm Lauren."

"I am sorry, Lauren," he repeated, the blue-green eyes pleading his case. "We're going to be working together closely over the next few weeks. I hope you won't hold this against me."

"Believe it or not, I completely understand your reaction. If I'd walked into an office and found the boss's daughter asleep and had no idea why, I'd have made the same call."

Well, maybe not. He probably considered her a spoiled woman who took advantage of her parents and in that, Lauren couldn't deny there was a hint of truth. At an age where most young women had moved on in their lives, had their own apartments and homes, careers, friends, and relationships, Lauren lived with her parents, worked for the family business, and pretty much depended on their support for her day-to-day existence.

It wasn't so much that she was unwilling to give those things a try. It required finding people who weren't scared off by her neediness.

She drew in a deep breath and sat down at her desk. "Let's start over. Tell me why you stopped by."

"Your father said you'd be able to provide me with the relevant data I'll need for my analysis. I want to go over the figures and do some charts and graphs to see if the situation relates to the economy or started further back."

"It shouldn't be any problem. All our records are computerized." She named a popular accounting program.

Jake nodded with satisfaction. "I'm familiar with that, so once I have computer access I should be able to pull the data for myself. I will need your expertise, though."

Lauren leaned forward and said, "I'm willing to do everything possible to help my parents improve and expand their business."

"Which will one day become your business," Jake pointed out. "Your father indicated he wants to keep the company going for you."

A wry smile touched her lips. "My great-grandfather started the company, and I'd love to see Sleep Dreams become a legacy for the future generations." The double-edged sword was that there was no one to continue Sleep Dreams after she was gone.

He stood and Lauren did the same. She shook his

outstretched hand. "It's been a pleasure meeting you, Jake."

They assessed each other for several seconds before he spoke. "I look forward to working together."

Strangely, despite her earlier embarrassment and humiliation, Lauren felt the same.

After he left, Lauren settled back in her chair. She'd been doing so much better, hadn't suffered an attack in a couple of days. And now she had to deal with Jake Greer's knowledge of her condition and his discomfort over calling her out, not to mention her own embarrassment.

Lauren should be used to it by now, but she didn't think she'd ever overcome the shame of being imperfect. Despite counseling sessions too numerous to count, she'd been unable to get past the pain caused by people thinking her lazy and unmotivated.

She was different but wanted to be normal. Not someone people avoided because they didn't know how to deal with her medical condition. She desired the same things as other women, and God willing, she hoped to one day have some semblance of a life. But on days like today, her condition made that nearly impossible. She had a good idea stress had brought on this attack.

Earlier in the year, her father had surprised them with his plan to solicit proposals for an efficiency study of their company. His friend had recently done the same and convinced Greg Kingsley he would benefit from the experience. Out of the six proposals received, he'd chosen Jacob Greer. As he shared information on the man he hoped would shift their financial picture deeper into the black, Lauren fought her body's natural reaction to the overwhelming onslaught of emotions.

Three generations of the Kingsley family had owned and operated Sleep Dreams, each improving product and profits. As chief financial officer, she looked at their financial dealings every day. Profits were down a small percentage, but she attributed that to rising costs and a drop in sales that had to do with the economy. Of course, some items her father mentioned were outside her control, such as the need to replace equipment and a possible expansion into a larger nearby city. Had she missed some key factor that impacted their business?

Lauren knew her father believed Jacob Greer could provide a fresh vision for their company. He certainly seemed dedicated to the cause. Enough to call her father on a daughter who slept on the job. She couldn't help but smile at that.

Her father's choice in a consultant intrigued her. From his proposal, it seemed he preferred challenging jobs where he could utilize his education to make the most impact for the company. Based on the references they'd received, he'd unerringly done that without fail for a number of satisfied customers.

And he wasn't hard on the eyes either. Though Jake wore his executive suit with style, he appeared to be a man more at home in casual clothes. Tall and broad in the shoulders, he couldn't claim washboard abs. Like her, he could afford to lose a few pounds, but not doing so wouldn't stop women from finding him attractive.

She guessed that like her, he was in his late twenties. He wore his dark hair in a short cut that required little attention. The dark beard made it appear he sported a five o'clock shadow all the time.

Her father had mentioned he planned to bring a child with him. A little boy named Teddy. What was the story behind that? Why did Jacob Greer travel alone with his son? Where was his wife?

Jake had hoped she wouldn't hold his snap judgment against him. She on the other hand hoped he wouldn't hold her condition against her.

❧

That afternoon Jake left the office in time to pick up Teddy and Yapper from their respective day cares. Now that he knew the lay of the land and felt comfortable with the job he'd signed up for, he really needed to find a home and a nanny. His job often required hours of overtime, and he needed to know they were safe and content. And he knew it would be cheaper than shelling out to the individual care facilities not to mention the hotel.

When the request for a proposal for this job came in, Jake thought about how he could make this work. He wasn't about to leave Teddy behind. Not while they were grieving Gwen's loss. His son needed his remaining parent.

After Gwen's death, his mother and stepfather had stayed at the house with Teddy while he completed his contract. When that wrapped up, he refused a couple of jobs until he could make some decisions about their future.

At first the idea of coming to North Carolina's Crystal Coast for a job hadn't seemed right for them. Then he'd gone onto the Internet and learned about the area. He'd accepted the job and brought his son and their dog to Morehead City in late July.

He collected Teddy and Yapper and headed for the hotel. Luckily, he'd found a place that allowed pets even if he did have to pay an extra fee. He really should pick up something for dinner. Did he have sufficient diapers for Teddy? Food for Teddy and Yapper? Formula?

Jake missed Gwen even more on days like this. When she'd been alive, he'd felt comfortable in the knowledge that their family was well cared for at home by a mother who loved them. Now he depended on the kindness of strangers for their care and faced an entirely different set of chores after work.

After stopping to pick up a burger, Jake drove to the hotel and parked. He found the room card, and then gathered baby, diaper bag, dog carrier, briefcase, and fast-food bag. Jake thanked the woman who held the elevator door for him. At the room door, he juggled everything and inserted the key. He left Yapper in her carrier and placed Teddy in the borrowed hotel crib while he changed into shorts and a T-shirt.

"Hey, buddy. Ready for dinner?" His son babbled agreement, reaching out to him. "Give me a minute." Jake went into the bathroom and washed his hands before coming back out to sort through the small jars on the countertop. He brewed a pot of coffee and carried the cup along with the baby food to the table.

He secured the bib and lifted Teddy from the crib, settling him in his lap. "Daddy might have messed up today," he told his son. "I upset the boss's daughter."

Teddy babbled "*dadadada*" in return.

"Yeah, it was stupid of me," he agreed, his thoughts drifting as he fed his son.

Lauren Kingsley had said she wouldn't hold it against him, but Jake knew he'd have to earn their respect back and that wasn't going to be easy. Why hadn't they told him? Surely they'd known something could happen.

After Teddy finished eating, Jake put him back into the crib while he ate his dinner. He considered the things he needed to do, like take Yapper for a walk and get Teddy ready for bed and go over some files he'd brought home. He rubbed one hand over his face, already bone weary.

By the time he went to bed that night, he was exhausted. Teddy slept and for once Yapper was quiet. Jake turned off the lamp and lay there, his thoughts a jumble of all that had happened that day. Sleep would not come and he tossed and turned, angry at himself for getting off on the wrong foot with the Kingsleys.

He called himself a troubleshooter, but today he'd been a troublemaker.

two

After a restless night, Jake called to request a meeting with Lauren. She welcomed him and asked Ashleigh to bring him a cup of coffee. She had a bottle of water.

"I think we need to address this elephant in the room."

"Excuse me." She looked stunned by his bluntness.

Jake forged on. "Let's talk about what happened yesterday."

"Why?" Lauren bracketed the question with the spread of her hands. "You didn't know and now you do. I don't hold grudges, Jake. I've lived with this long enough to understand how senseless that would be."

"Tell me about narcolepsy." He truly wanted to know.

"It's a neurological sleep disorder, triggered by the brain's inability to regulate sleep-wake cycles normally. Third most frequently diagnosed sleep disorder."

"How does it affect you?"

"I suffer from overwhelming daytime sleepiness. As for sleeping on the job, I do take brief naps, which help me stay more alert. Yesterday was a full-blown sleep attack. I think the stress of your arrival and my underlying fear that the company is in trouble might have triggered the situation."

"Your dad is being proactive, Lauren. He brought me in to help him look at the bottom line, to find ways to improve the operation. I hate feeling I got off on the wrong foot with Greg. Being a parent myself, I should have known better."

"Than to address a concern with the heir apparent?" she mocked, a smile curving her lips. "We discussed this last night. Daddy says we're at fault for not filling you in."

He placed his cup on the desk. "And I was equally at fault for jumping to conclusions."

Jake had noted Lauren talked with her hands. Now she lifted her palms out toward him. "So let's put it behind us and move on with business."

"Can we do that?" Jake asked. "I mean. . .I don't know much. . . . Actually I don't know anything about narcolepsy."

"Wish I could say the same." Lauren sounded morose.

"It's bad?"

"Life altering. At least my father is an understanding boss."

Jake paused for a minute and said, "I saw your emotional battle yesterday."

"Chaos and anguish," she joked. "That's my life."

Jake appreciated her attempt to bring humor into what must be a devastating situation. "I'm sorry I added to your worries."

"Don't be. Believe it or not, I'm blessed and I know it. I have loving parents who work hard to help make a difference in my life."

"You were born with this?"

She shook her head. "The symptoms started when I was around ten. Eventually the doctors did a sleep study and I was diagnosed. I'm the one in two thousand."

He waited for her to continue.

"Narcolepsy steals your life and your dignity. Doesn't matter what you're doing when the episodes occur. Having people laugh at me or comment that I'm lazy doesn't help."

Jake felt sufficiently chastened. He'd lost sleep over his insensitive behavior. "I'm sorry."

"I didn't mean you," she told him. "The medication and scheduled naps help me function as normally as I can."

No doubt the disorder caused her great anguish. He made a mental note to do research. He wanted to know more.

Jake hoped she didn't take his inquiry the wrong way. "Is there anything I should do if you have an attack while we're together?"

Lauren shrugged. "Do what you can to help me avoid injury."

"I appreciate you telling me this."

Her brow creased with worry. "Please keep the information to yourself. It's not common knowledge within the company."

Jake nodded agreement.

"Daddy tells me you have a little boy."

Jake pulled out his wallet and handed her a photo. "That's Teddy. He's eight months old."

"Oh how sweet. He's precious."

He noted the way she stared at the photo with something like longing in her gaze before handing it back.

"Thank you." He glanced down at the baby with his big grin and his mom's silky blond hair. Jake knew the color would probably change over time, but for now it was very blond. "He can be a handful at times."

"From what I've heard, they all are."

"We lost his mom this past February."

"I'm sorry."

He appreciated her obvious sincerity. "It's been difficult but we're getting by."

And they were. Some days were more difficult than others, but their routine fell into place and Jake found it comforting.

Jake felt more in control when he left Lauren's office. And true to her word, the Kingsleys didn't hold his gaffe against him. In fact, Jake found Lauren's disorder had very little effect on the work she performed. She came in with her father every morning and stayed until after six or seven most days.

She was a fount of knowledge regarding the company. More often than not, Greg Kingsley sent him to Lauren for answers.

He hadn't witnessed any further sleep attacks when they were together, but then Lauren spent the majority of her days sequestered in her office. Was she so concerned about others witnessing her attacks that she would imprison herself rather than risk someone finding out? While curious, he wouldn't ask.

❧

"Hey, Mom, what's up?" Lauren caught the phone between her shoulder and ear as she replaced the ribbon in her calculator.

"I invited Jake and Teddy to dinner tonight. Make sure you and your father get home on time."

Lauren held back a sigh. Wasn't it enough that she spent numerous hours of each day with Jake? Now her mother expected her to entertain him as well.

She liked him, but he made her feel unsettled. She had reached a comfort zone with her problem and contented herself with the life she had. Evidently Jake found the subject interesting enough to do his own research, and at times she felt like a bug under a microscope. He watched her so closely that she wondered if he was waiting for the next attack.

"Laurie, did you hear me?"

She could hear kitchen sounds. "Yes, Mom. I'll make sure we're home before six. You say he's bringing Teddy?"

"And their dog. He can't leave her behind because he's afraid her barking would cause problems at the hotel. He actually refused for that reason, but I told him to bring Yapper, too."

The name brought a smile to Lauren's face. She wondered who named the animal. Certainly two faces of Jake—father and furry little pet owner. He'd told her the dog was a teacup Yorkie Terrier. Not exactly a man's dog.

Despite her mixed feelings, Lauren looked forward to meeting his son and uncovering another facet of Jacob Greer. "We'll be home in plenty of time." Then another thought popped into her head. "Mom, has Jake ever said anything about what happened to his wife?"

"She drowned. Really sad, her dying like that and leaving

behind a tiny baby. Jake explained the situation to your father when he called to offer him the job."

Lauren replaced the receiver and went to wash the ink from her fingertips. Back at her desk, she tried to concentrate on the work at hand, but her mind wandered.

She wished her life had more facets. There were two—daughter and CFO for her father's company. Actually there was another more important one—child of God. She loved the Lord and knew He would take care of her no matter what happened. That was one truth she could rely upon.

Her childhood had been a normal one. She'd been an adored only child and grandchild. Like any child's, her life had its ups and downs, bumps and bruises, but for the most part she'd been happy. She did all the normal kid stuff, attended school, played with her friends, and had sleepovers. And then everything changed.

The narcolepsy had been diagnosed, and they had come to accept things would never improve for her. She took medication and learned what would help her stay awake. And told herself her life was the best it would ever be.

☙

At seven on the dot, Lauren opened the front door to find Jake juggling his son, pet carrier, and diaper bag. Teddy immediately threw out his arms toward Lauren. She smiled and touched his hand. "Hey there, cutie. Here, let me help you with that."

Taking the pet carrier that looked more like an expensive purse from Jake, Lauren noted his surprise. She knew he expected her to take the baby, but she was too inexperienced with children to take the risk.

She set the carrier on the floor and unzipped it. A tiny excited ball of fur exited and ran from the entry hall.

"Yapper," Jake called. "Come here."

His stern tone yielded no response.

"I didn't mean for her to run free." Jake placed the diaper

bag on the chair and took a step in the direction Yapper had gone.

"She's okay." Lauren grabbed the diaper bag and took his arm. "Fred's in the family room with Daddy. Come on back."

Jake frowned. "Who is Fred?"

"Daddy's dog."

They walked into the open plan kitchen, dining, and family room to find the old bloodhound on his feet growling at the little dog.

"Fred, quiet," her father ordered.

Her mother chuckled as the little dog stood her ground against the larger and older bloodhound. She glanced at Jake. "I take it this is Yapper?"

He nodded. "Yes, ma'am. I'll put her back in the carrier." Jake shifted Teddy and reached for the dog that remained just out of his grasp.

Seeing his frustration, Lauren looked at her mom and said, "I told him she's okay."

"Let her be," Suzanne dismissed with a wave of her hand. "Fred's bark is worse than his bite. I'm sure they'll be best friends before the night is over." She held out a hand. "I'm Suzanne."

He shifted Teddy and reached out. "Jake."

With all the excitement, Teddy bounced in his father's arms.

"Hello, sweetie," Suzanne said. She reached for him and then asked, "May I?"

Jake handed over his son. "He's absolutely adorable," she exclaimed. Teddy gave her a big grin. "How old are you, pretty boy?"

"*Dadadada.*" The baby pointed to his father.

"Eight months."

Lauren watched her mother with Teddy. Lauren had never been around babies. She'd missed out on babysitting in her teens, and there had been no siblings or cousins to practice on. Her mother's necklace caught his attention, and he reached for the twinkling diamond. Her mother took the delicate chain from his fingers and dropped it into her shirt. The baby searched for the hidden object, and he worked his fingers indicating he wanted her necklace.

"Isn't he sweet, Laurie?"

She nodded. "Yes, ma'am. He's quite the handsome fellow."

The pasta pot boiled over, and Lauren hurried over to handle the situation. After dinner was under control, she found treats for the dogs.

"Here you go, Freddie." She tossed the treat, and the dog barely moved as he snapped it up.

Lauren broke the other treat into smaller pieces and offered them to Yapper who ate more daintily. Soon the two dogs stretched out together on the cool hardwood floor.

When his son started to cry, Jake stood. "I need to feed him. I planned to do it before we came over but ended up making a grocery run after I picked them up."

Suzanne held Teddy while he washed up and pulled jars of peas and applesauce from the diaper bag. He added a spoon and bottle of formula. "Seems no matter how much of this stuff I buy we're always running out."

"Let me have that." Suzanne passed the baby over and took the bottle. "I'll warm it for him."

Jake sat at the island and tied a bib about his son's neck before he opened the jar of peas.

Lauren noted things like the food was cold and there was no plate. He must feed the baby straight from the jar. "Would you like me to heat those up for you?" She indicated the peas.

He pushed the jar in her direction. "Sure. Not long though, or it'll be too hot."

He popped the seal on the applesauce, and the lid clattered on the island. The baby devoured half the container before she returned with the warmed peas in a bowl. Teddy made faces when the food changed.

"Not the same is it, buddy?" Jake asked when he spooned the warm peas into Teddy's mouth.

"He's a good eater," Suzanne said.

"We do lots of food testing. There's some stuff he won't eat. Hates mixed peas and carrots."

Lauren noted her mother's nostalgic expression. "Remember those sessions with Laurie?" she asked her husband.

He smiled and nodded.

"She wasn't picky at all. The problems started when she decided to feed herself. She rubbed food all through her hair and tossed the bowl onto the floor when she'd had enough. I had to bathe her after every meal."

Jake glanced at Lauren. "You wild woman, you."

Suzanne winked at her daughter. "Thankfully, her table manners have improved by leaps and bounds."

Jake gave Teddy his bottle and he soon fell asleep. He cradled his son comfortably in his arms.

"Dinner's ready," Suzanne announced as she placed the platter on the table. She turned an oversized armchair toward the table and folded a throw from the sofa. "Lay him here, Jake. We'll use this chair to block him in case he rolls."

Over the meal, the conversation turned to Jake's first impressions of their business. "You have a quality product and the custom mattresses are a good idea. You need more promotion."

Greg scooped spaghetti onto his plate and added the chicken Parmesan. "Laurie suggested that awhile back. A local channel wanted to do a segment, but I never got around to scheduling it."

"Getting yourself out there in the public eye will make a difference," Jake pointed out. "A mattress is an investment. The public wants the best. You have to show them it's your product."

"Suzanne's better at that kind of thing."

"You could do it, Greg."

Jake cut into the chicken breast and took a bite. "Delicious," he told Suzanne. "You should check with them and see if they're still interested. Free publicity is good."

Lauren grinned when Yapper came over and jumped up, her paws resting on Jake's leg.

"Guess you forgot to feed somebody."

He frowned and nodded. "I got food for her, too. She'll have to eat out of the can."

No feminine touches for the Greer family, Lauren thought. She placed her napkin on the table and went to rummage in the utility room off the kitchen. Lauren returned with a bowl. "This should work."

"That's real china," Jake protested, pushing the fragile saucer back at her.

"Old set we don't use anymore," she explained. "I managed to break most of the pieces, so we got new dishes."

"If you're sure?" His expression told her he wasn't.

"Where's her food?"

He retrieved a small can from the diaper bag and popped the lid. He plunked it into the dish and added a little dry food from a plastic bag. Dismayed by the glob of food, Lauren asked, "Don't you cut it up for her?"

He shrugged. "She eats around the edges until it's gone."

Lauren used a plastic spoon to make the food more appetizing. "There, that's better." She set the bowl on the floor and patted Yapper's tiny head. She barked and nibbled daintily at the miniature dog–sized bites.

They washed their hands and returned to the table.

"I knew we'd be trouble when you invited us to dinner," Jake told Suzanne.

"Not at all. It's been a pleasure meeting your family. What do you do with Teddy and Yapper during the day?"

"Day care until I make other arrangements. I hope to find someone to keep them both."

Greg helped himself to a second serving of cheese bread. "You could bring Teddy to the office."

Jake shook his head. "He demands my attention when we're together. Hard to accomplish anything with a crying baby in tow." He turned the conversation back to plans for the business. "How's employee morale? Have the employees had a recent raise?"

Lauren sipped her tea. "We managed a longevity percentage last Christmas. It was based on their years with the company."

"What was their reaction?"

She glanced at her father and back at Jake and shrugged. "I think they were happy. Most have been with us long enough that it was a decent amount. Enough to offset their Christmas expenses."

"What other perks do they have? Do they promote Sleep Dreams to their family and friends?"

"Regular benefits. Vacation and sick leave. Good health care plan. And most of them have purchased a mattress from the company." Again Lauren glanced at her dad for confirmation. He nodded. "They get a discount on any mattresses they purchase. And a twenty-five-dollar bonus for any referrals that result in a sale if the purchaser gives their name."

Jake nodded. "You say they've been with you for a while?"

"Oh yes," Suzanne said. "A number of them worked for Greg's father. Some have retired and now their children work for us."

"Have you addressed succession planning?"

Greg nodded. "We do considerable cross training. Older employees work with the younger ones on a regular basis."

"Do their benefits include retirement?"

"We match up to three percent of what they're putting into their plans. Most take advantage of the offer," Lauren said.

Greg smiled at his wife. "Delicious meal, Suze." She patted his hand.

Suzanne stood and took her own and Greg's plate to the sink.

"Finished?" Lauren asked, taking Jake's when he nodded.

Her mother picked up the cake stand from the counter. Lauren brought over the dessert plates.

"A number of small companies have been forced to reduce benefits to help their profit margins."

"We've had to pass on some increases to our employees," Greg admitted, thanking his wife for the slice of cake. "Mainly health insurance, but we'd like to avoid cuts if possible."

Jake took the plate Lauren passed him. "What about layoffs? Have you considered the possibility if sales drop?"

"We'll consider our options if the worst happens," Greg said without hesitation.

"You need to review those options now, Greg. See how benefits figure into the bottom line. You can't wait until you're in trouble."

Greg sighed heavily.

Lauren felt for her father. His generosity would have far-reaching effects on the company's bottom line. If someone didn't act as the voice of reason, he'd give the workers the shirt off his back.

"Lauren has an idea for an advertisement," Suzanne told Jake. "She wants to set up a bed on the beach, one of those iron canopy beds with sheer curtains blowing in the breeze. There's a couple asleep on a Sleep Dreams mattress with peaceful smiles while the waves roll in and out." She looked at Lauren. "What was your slogan?"

"Make every night as restful as a tropical vacation," she offered tentatively.

Jake's brows shot up with approval. "I like it. Let's see what we can do with that."

Teddy woke, and her mom rose from the table and took him into the family room. From his laughter, Lauren knew the baby was happy.

Jake insisted on helping with the dishes. They loaded and started the dishwasher. Jake wiped the dinner table, pushing the crumbs into his hand. Rinsing the dishcloth, he folded it over the sink divider. They picked up their tea glasses and joined the others.

Yapper tormented Fred until he snapped at her.

"He's going to eat her alive if she keeps that up."

"He won't hurt her," Lauren said. "Fred knows she's a puppy."

Jake shook his head. "She's three years old."

"But she's so little," Lauren said, picking Yapper up and cuddling her. "The perfect size to carry around. She can't weigh more than four or five pounds."

"She fit into the palm of my hand when we first got her. One of Gwen's girlfriends had a pup and she had to have one."

Lauren pulled the hair about the dog's face up into a little ponytail. "You should tie it up with a pink bow."

Jake grimaced. "I don't think so."

Lauren grinned. "She's a girl. We like pink. Don't we?" The dog yipped in agreement.

"All that hair is a pain. I have to brush her several times a week or it gets matted. Honestly, it's like having two little kids to care for. At times, she demands more attention than Teddy.

"You should see her wardrobe," he continued. "Gwen insisted clothes were a necessity because Yapper got cold easily."

That surprised Lauren. She thought of the times she'd played dress up with her dolls. His wife had done the same with their dog. "You dress her?"

"No way. I left them in a box in my uncle's garage. Yapper's going au naturel with me."

The conversation picked up again and around eight thirty, Jake said it was time to go. He packed up and took Teddy from Suzanne.

"Thanks for the wonderful dinner. Best meal I've had in a while."

"Thank you. Come again soon. I've enjoyed spending time with you and Teddy. And Yapper."

Lauren stood and said, "I'll help you get everything to the car."

She carried Yapper and paused in the kitchen to pick up the bag of goodies her mother had packed for Jake to have later.

In the entry hall, Lauren gave the dog a final pat before placing her in the carrier. She grabbed the handle and led the way to his vehicle.

She opened the back door and secured Yapper's bag with a seat belt as Jake fastened Teddy into his car seat. Lauren set the food on the floorboard. "Don't forget this."

Jake grinned and said, "It probably won't make it into the fridge."

She looked at him and asked, "Is Sleep Dreams in trouble?"

"That's why I'm here," Jake said. "To ensure it never is."

three

"Good morning."

Jake entered her office at eight a.m. on Monday morning carrying two large cups of coffee. "Caramel mocha," he said, placing one on her desk. "Do you have time to review a couple of reports later this morning?"

Lauren looked at the cup with longing before she smiled and pushed it back at him. "Sorry, only water or decaf coffee and tea for me. I'm available around eleven. Will that work?"

He pulled up his calendar on his phone and nodded. "Looks good. We can have lunch in the cafeteria."

"Ashleigh can have them bring something to my office," Lauren offered.

Jake shook his head. "You need to eat with the employees whenever possible. Open a dialogue with them, improve operations and morale."

"Daddy does. . ."

"Greg, too," Jake interrupted. "It's a family business, Lauren. Make them feel like part of your family and you'll reap the benefits."

Unconsciously her brow furrowed. "What if I have an attack? They'll be uncomfortable and so will I."

"You need to let them know about your condition."

Startled, Lauren declared, "No way. The fewer people who know, the better."

"It's nothing to be ashamed about."

"You don't understand. People look at you differently when they're aware of weird medical conditions." Poor, pitiful Lauren wasn't the way she wanted to live. "I don't want anyone feeling sorry for me. Particularly the people who work here. I have an image to uphold."

Jake stared at her. She wanted to turn away but couldn't.

"You're too proud to accept that someone might care you have this condition that forces you to hide yourself away from life?"

It had nothing to do with pride. She wanted people to care about her as a normal person.

Lauren glanced down at her desk, her voice low as she said, "People get weirded out when they witness others losing control. They don't know what to do so they turn their heads and later whisper about this pitiful woman who shouldn't be out in public."

He frowned. "Don't you just fall asleep?"

If only it were that simple. Maybe she should explain the variables associated with her condition. "Tell me it wouldn't freak you out if I fell asleep in the middle of this conversation. Maybe kept on writing or using the calculator while I appear to be asleep?"

"You can do that?"

Lauren nodded. "I've seen pads where I kept writing until it became illegible."

Her gaze shifted over the powerful set of his shoulders. How would he deal with the life she lived on a daily basis? Not much differently, she decided. Narcolepsy could drop a man his size as easily as it did her.

"Before I knew, maybe," Jake admitted. "Knowledge is power, Lauren. Making these people aware would offer you more protection. They wouldn't let anyone hurt you."

There were very few people she trusted with the knowledge that she wasn't always in control. She didn't fool herself that every employee relished the opportunity to help the boss's daughter through her sleep attacks. "How can you be so sure of that? People with narcolepsy have been taken advantage of when they were at their weakest. When I'm having an attack, I'm as helpless as Teddy. Would you hand him over to a stranger and expect them to take care of him?"

"No," he conceded.

"I have trust issues. Blame them on the school friends who fell into fits of giggles when I had an attack. Or to the guy who invited me to his prom and then deserted me. His girlfriend told him he was insensitive, and he got it into his head that inviting me to the prom would make her see him as more sensitive. I had to call Daddy to pick me up."

Jake grimaced. "I'm sorry, Lauren, but hiding yourself away from hurt isn't the answer. When you work through fiscal problems here at the plant, do you stop after one try? Or do you keep going until you find a solution?"

"I keep going."

He nodded. "You have to do the same with your life."

"I'm not sure I'm that strong. It hurts too much."

"So you'd rather have no life?"

She took a shaky breath. "I have a life, Jake."

"Do you really? You limited your world. Denied yourself the things you wanted. Told yourself you couldn't have them. What if you could?"

"And what if I can't?" The hazel eyes fixed on him. Challenging him to answer.

Impasse. He didn't understand her world. And she couldn't explain.

"You could take short jaunts into the cafeteria. Pick up the food yourself. Make a point of speaking to a different group of people each time."

Frustrated, Lauren asked, "Why don't you conduct a survey on their perception of our family? Of me?"

"And what if they think you feel you're too good to associate with them?"

"That's not fair."

He sighed. "They don't know why you hide from them."

"I don't hide."

Even with the strength of her denial, Lauren knew she

lied. She might tell herself that was the case, but she couldn't put herself out there for the world to point fingers at and mock. She'd experienced people laughing at her when she was at her most vulnerable. She never wanted to hear the sound again.

"Okay, Lauren. You have to decide when you're going to stop secreting yourself from the world. I'll be back at eleven."

He rose, took the second cup of coffee, and walked out, closing the door behind him.

That hurt. Despite the short time she'd known him, Lauren couldn't believe Jake would say that to her. He acted as though he understood, but he didn't. He'd never walked in her shoes, lived with her condition. He couldn't begin to understand the necessity of protecting yourself from hurt.

Hadn't her disorder destroyed her childhood friendships? Parents didn't want their children playing with kids who were liabilities. They didn't want the responsibility, and no matter how often her mother reassured them Lauren was the same girl she'd always been, they avoided her.

Over the years, Lauren and her mother had become best friends. They had done so much together. Her mom even accompanied her on the few trips she'd taken as an adult. Lauren sometimes wondered if her dad had felt pushed out of the relationship with his wife or accepted it had to be this way because she was his child, too. She worked hard not to come between her parents. Mostly she felt like a third wheel. She was always there, in the midst of their lives; everything they planned included her, just as it had when she was little. They wouldn't do anything without assuring themselves she was safe.

Perhaps she should go to the cafeteria with Jake, Lauren thought. What he'd said about secreting herself in her office hurt, but it was true. She was too afraid to risk divulging the truth about herself.

When he returned, Jake said nothing of their earlier

discussion. Lauren went over the reports in great detail, and they wrapped up their meeting a few minutes after noon.

"Thanks for your help. I needed to be sure I was interpreting the data correctly." He glanced at his watch. "Did Ashleigh order lunch?"

Lauren shook her head. "We're going to the cafeteria."

His penetrating blue-green gaze fixed on her. "Are you sure?"

She wished she felt as confident as Jake. "No."

"If you feel an attack coming on, let me know and I'll get you out of there."

"If there's time." Lauren left the comment open-ended. Though she usually recognized the signs of onset with an attack, she had no idea whether she could manage an escape once it started. "Look after me if it happens."

Jake appeared less confident.

She rose and walked around the desk. "Come on. Let's get this over with."

"You make it sound as though I'm doing something terrible to you," Jake protested.

Ashleigh was not at her desk. Lauren paused to write a note and stuck it on the phone.

"It's my decision," she told him.

"Because I pushed you?"

She didn't respond.

As they walked into the cafeteria, Jake said softly, "Remember, these people care about you and your family. They depend on you for their living. You need to learn to depend on them."

She sensed Jake appraising her interaction with the employees.

"These seats taken?" he asked the two men sitting at the large table.

"No," the older man said. "Help yourself."

Jake set the tray on the table and pulled out her chair.

"I'm Jacob Greer. I'm working with the Kingsleys to improve company production. You know Lauren Kingsley." The two men nodded in her direction. "We'd like to hear anything you'd care to share about the company."

It took a few minutes, but the two men eventually opened up. Mostly they sang praises for Sleep Dreams. "Best job I ever had," the man named Wade announced. "Fair salary, good working conditions, and people who care. Jimmy here had some health problems earlier in the year, and Mr. Kingsley called to check on him regularly. Asked if he needed help. Not many bosses willing to do that."

The men's comments boosted her spirits. When morale was low, the workers groused about their working environment. Her father preferred they be happy and content. Sometimes he went too far in his efforts to help them, but that was her dad.

The men stood and picked up their trays. "Need to get back to work. Nice meeting you, Mr. Greer. Good seeing you, Miss Lauren."

"Good seeing you, too, Wade, Jimmy."

The lunch break had passed quickly. When Jake opened her office door, he asked, "That wasn't so bad, was it?"

Tell that to my pounding heart, Lauren thought. "It wasn't bad."

"It gets easier with practice," Jake told her.

"Let's hope so."

"I've been thinking about the television program. Why didn't you offer to do the show?"

"Oh I couldn't," Lauren protested.

"Why not?"

"The stress. . ."

She couldn't begin to imagine how her condition would react to her doing something so out of line with her normal practices.

His brows lifted. "Are you afraid?"

"I'm not exactly the best spokesperson for Sleep Dreams."

His gaze shifted over her face. "You're attractive, personable, and well-spoken. I think you'd be the perfect person to do the show."

While she appreciated his compliments, Lauren couldn't believe he couldn't see the truth for himself. "It would be too stressful. Mom can do it. She's good at things like that."

Jake shrugged and said, "Someone should. Any promotion is good for your company."

"I plan to call and ask if they're still interested."

He nodded. "Do you have any customer testimonials on file?"

"We have mail. And the comments on the website. They're positive for the most part. A couple of disgruntled customers, but that's to be expected."

"I'd like to see them."

"I'll have Ashleigh bring the file to you." She walked into her office, thinking Jake would leave. He stuck his head back inside and asked, "Can you stay late tonight? I need your help with the accounts."

"What about Teddy?"

"I made arrangements for him to stay late at day care. Yapper's overnighting at the doggie care place."

"Sure. How late? I'll tell Daddy so he can pick me up."

"I can drive you home."

Lauren smiled. "I'm sure he'll appreciate not having to come back out. It's times like this when I wish I had my license."

"What's stopping you?"

The question hammered at her. She told him the truth. "I never learned to drive."

"Would they give you a license?"

"If a doctor signed off that I'm okay to drive."

"I'll teach you if you like."

Stunned, Lauren said, "I'll pray about it."

He nodded. "Good idea. Where do you attend church?"

"Peace."

"I'd like to find a church home for Teddy and myself."

It pleased her that Jake was a believer. "You're welcome anytime. We have a large nursery. Teddy would be happy there."

"Give me the address," he requested.

❧

"Jake offered to teach me to drive," Lauren announced when she came into the family room that night.

Her parents looked at each other and back at her.

Lauren held up one hand. "I know what you're thinking, but I checked and I can have a driver's license as long as my narcolepsy is under control. I think I might like to give it a try. Daddy, will you help me find a cheap used car to drive? I don't want to risk damaging Jake's vehicle."

"Use my old truck," he suggested.

"Are you sure? You love that truck."

"I love you more. So don't dent yourself."

Lauren chuckled. "That's the plan. Jake says we'll find a secluded road so I can get plenty of practice."

"You could drive around the farm," her mother said. "I learned on those dirt roads surrounding the fields. I doubt you'll find anywhere more secluded."

Lauren hadn't visited the farm since her grandmother passed away a few months earlier. "That's perfect. Jake says he'll find a babysitter. I told him I'd pay."

"Have him bring them over," her mother said. "I'll babysit in exchange for your driving lessons."

Lauren met her mother's smile with one of her own. "I will. I invited him to church. Told him I needed to pray over learning to drive, and he said it was a good idea. Even if I master driving, I have to consider what could happen if I experienced an attack while behind the wheel."

"Why haven't you ever told us you wanted to learn to drive?"

She shrugged. "I suppose this is one of those times when I thought why not instead of no way."

four

On Saturday, Jake drove them out to the farm. Lauren directed him to the shed where her father parked his old truck. When he'd gone to trade vehicles, the dealership hadn't offered him much in a trade-in and he opted to keep the truck. Her mother used it occasionally for work, and they loaned it to friends when their vehicles were out of service.

As she stood in the farmyard, memories of the times she'd spent here flooded Lauren. She'd played with the cats and dog in this yard, swung in the old white swing in the garden, and climbed the old tree by the house, though she'd been too afraid to climb back down. She'd ridden the fields on her grandfather's tractor and wandered the farm in exploration.

Later, when fear kept her closer to home, the adults encouraged Lauren to come see the new farm animals and explore. She missed her friends and didn't understand the changes, but they did everything they could to make her life as normal as possible.

"You ready?"

She turned back to where Jake stood and nodded. Once in the truck, he followed Lauren's directions, and they bumped along the dirt and grass track running alongside the field. Jake parked underneath the big tree Lauren knew had shaded farmers for many generations.

"First, I need to teach you the basics."

He unhooked his seat belt and leaned closer to remove the manual from the glove compartment. As Jake covered the various components of the truck, Lauren grew impatient. "I know all this."

He appeared doubtful. Lauren wondered if his behavior would

be stereotypical of parents teaching their children to drive.

"I do," she repeated. "I read all the time. I read the manual years ago while waiting on Daddy."

"That's good, but we're doing this my way. Sometimes manuals are not clear, and I want to be sure you understand."

She frowned at him and Jake laughed. "Stop that or I'll think you're not old enough to learn how to drive."

Lauren paid attention and repeated the information to his satisfaction. Jake opened the door and climbed out.

"Okay, slide behind the wheel. Adjust the mirrors and seat so you're comfortable."

Suddenly her palms grew moist. "Ah, Jake, maybe. . ."

"Come on, Lauren. Don't chicken out on me now. You can do this."

She slipped across the seat and sat stiffly behind the steering wheel. Was she doing the right thing? She looked at Jake again. He wasn't going to let her back out. He told her to fasten her seat belt, and went around to the passenger side. He settled in the middle of the bench seat.

Very aware of his presence, Lauren mumbled, "There's no seat belt there."

"We won't get ticketed back here."

"True, but I'd feel better knowing you're secure."

His eyes were gentle, understanding. "And I need to be able to take the wheel or hit the brake pedal if you lose control. I can't do that over there."

She pulled a face. "Okay, but hold on."

Their arms brushed and Lauren drew in a deep breath, so aware of him she could hardly concentrate.

"Check your mirrors and turn your head to look behind you. It never hurts to walk around the vehicle to check for kids and pets. Okay, turn the ignition key."

The truck started up immediately.

"Now place your foot on the brake pedal and pull the gear lever into drive."

He leaned closer and pointed to the *D* indicator on the column. Lauren drew a deep breath. If he came any closer, he was going to push her out of the vehicle.

"Now give it some gas." Jake's soft command seemed to brush her ear. The vehicle surged forward.

"Lightly," he yelped.

Lauren jammed the brake pedal, jerking them forward again.

Jake touched his neck and said, "Slow and easy, Lauren."

Calm down, she told herself. *You can do this.*

She gripped the steering wheel and focused on keeping the truck on the road. A thrill of excitement filled her when they crept along the grass and dirt track.

Their journey moved from slow to fast as she struggled to adjust her foot on the accelerator. Driving and ignoring Jake took every bit of Lauren's concentration. One time he grabbed the wheel when she hit a rut and bounced out of the tracks and into the edge of the field.

"Okay, let's turn around. See that layby up ahead? When you get closer, pull over and turn around."

She did as he instructed. Jake seemed as surprised as Lauren when the wheels sank into the sandy soil. He groaned and climbed out to find the rear tires buried.

"Let's see if we can free ourselves. I'll push. You drive forward."

Lauren drew a deep breath and pressed the gas. The tires slung sand everywhere, and Jake yelled for her to stop. She jerked her foot from the pedal.

He stepped back, brushing sand from his face and hair. "Put it in reverse. Let's see if we can rock it back and forth."

Lauren was terrified. "I've got my phone. I can call Daddy," she yelled out the open window.

"Come on, Lauren. Trust me. We can do this," Jake shouted back.

Determination raised his chin and fired his gaze. This sand

wasn't about to stop him. His tenacity came as no surprise. It had been so long since she trusted anyone but her parents. Lauren pressed the gas pedal and moved the truck backward.

"That's good. Do it again."

She clutched the steering wheel, the tips of her fingers white with strain. The truck moved a bit farther.

"Okay, put it in drive and gun it."

The engine strained as if bound by some mighty force. Jake jumped clear of the truck.

"Good job," he yelled after she drove several feet down the road before stopping.

Lauren shoved the gear into park, released her seat belt, and climbed out. Jake grabbed her close, and her feet left the ground as he swung her about. "You did it. You got the truck out."

"You pushed."

He shook his head. "Not that last time when you reversed and then went forward. You shot out of there like a rocket. Ready to continue?"

Wobbly from the experience, she shook her head. "I think I've done enough for my first attempt."

"You have to get back into the driver's seat when something like this happens. I'll turn the truck around and you can drive back to the end of the road."

She drove all the way back to the house and stopped in the driveway.

He touched her shoulder. "Good job, Lauren. You're a natural."

She didn't believe that for one minute. Right now, all she could think was that she'd not had an attack during a stressful situation.

Jake studied the small frame house and asked, "Who lives here?"

"No one. It was my grandparents' home. Gramps died a couple of years ago and Gram a few months back."

The house gleamed white with the fresh coat of paint it had received at the first of the summer. The trim was crimson red. Her mother planned to fix the house up and rent it out. The land had been leased to another farmer earlier in the year by her grandmother.

"Nice place."

"Come on inside. There's soda in the fridge."

Lauren opened the door with a key on the ring she carried. They stepped into the sunny kitchen. Boxes littered the room where her mom had attempted to begin the process of going through her parents' possessions.

Taking two bottles from the ancient fridge, Lauren passed him one and twisted off the cap of the other one. She pulled a chair about and sat down at the table.

"Mind if I look at the rest of the place?" Jake asked.

She stood. "I'll give you the nickel tour."

The house was small by most people's standards. An eat-in kitchen, living room, den, two bedrooms, and a bath and three-quarters. Her grandfather had converted a section of the wraparound porch into a combination mudroom/bathroom for them, leaving the original bathroom for their daughter.

"Mom's room," Lauren announced, indicating the small room. "You should have seen it before she had it painted. It was a very rich, royal purple. Her favorite color. I slept in here when I stayed with them. I liked the color, too."

"Perfect size room for a kid." He glanced around again. "You think your mom would consider renting the place short-term? It would be great for us. And I could help with the renovation. I'm a good painter."

Lauren studied him closely, realizing he was serious. "You could ask. Though I think it might be awhile before she sorts through everything. Mom's finding it hard going at this stage. I suggested she leave the house empty or let us put their things in storage until she's ready."

"I think I will ask. I could see us fitting in here. We can

live with things just as they are."

They locked the house, and Jake parked her dad's truck back in the shed. They didn't talk much on the ride home. Lauren unlocked the door to her parents' Front Street historical home, and they went inside. Her mother was in the family room.

Suzanne looked up from the house photos on her laptop. "How did it go?"

"She did great," Jake enthused.

Lauren pointed out somewhat dryly, "I got us bogged down in a field."

"But we got out," Jake said.

"Optimist," Lauren muttered.

Suzanne laughed. "I'm glad it went well. Fred and Yapper need to be walked."

Lauren went to get the bloodhound's leash and met Jake at the door of the family room. "You want to take Teddy?"

"He's asleep," Suzanne said. "Poor little guy had a miserable afternoon. He's teething."

Jake grimaced. "Sorry."

Suzanne nodded. "I gave him an ice cube in a cloth and it seemed to help."

"Really? I'll pick up a teething ring. And some baby acetaminophen. That reminds me. I need a pediatrician. Any suggestions?" He took the leash from Lauren and knelt to secure it to Fred's collar. He patted the dog. "Come on, fella. Time for a walk."

Everyone chuckled when the old dog's expression seemed to be something less than approval.

"Laurie's pediatrician is still practicing. I can give you the name and number."

"This parenting stuff is a challenge. Gwen handled everything."

"You're doing fine," Suzanne said. "Parenting is a learn-as-you-go process. No manuals for kids."

Jake feigned surprise. "Don't tell me that. I get all my development stuff off the Internet."

Suzanne burst into laughter. "Just don't get paranoid if he doesn't do something when the experts say he should. Kids develop at their own pace."

Lauren felt an overwhelming desire to have her mother share information with her regarding a grandchild. A child she might never be able to provide. Yapper barked and Fred growled.

"Come on, Jake. We'll be back soon, Mom," she said, feeling suddenly anxious to escape their conversation.

"Want to stay for dinner?" Suzanne called over her shoulder.

He paused and grinned back at her. "You know I can't turn down a home-cooked meal. If I never saw another container of takeout or fast food, I wouldn't care."

"We'll throw together a meal when you get back."

They let themselves out the side door and walked around to the sidewalk. Jake studied her parents' two-storied house with two porches and a widow's walk. "I like this house."

"It's been said Beaufort architecture was influenced by that of the Bahamas. Planters built their summer homes here to escape the heat and conduct their sea-related endeavors. Mostly wooden construction and white paint. The houses were often built by shipwrights. They knew how to build a house to stand up to the weather."

Across Front Street, past the sidewalk and piers, Taylor Creek sparkled and flashed like diamonds in the sunlight.

"Here," Jake said, passing her Yapper's leash. "You take her. I'll take Fred."

"You worried that good old Fred's gonna drag me down the street?" Lauren chuckled at the thought. "Or that someone will challenge your manhood because of your sissy dog?"

"Fred needs a stronger hand than Yapper."

This time Lauren roared with laughter. "Fat chance. He ambles along without a care in the world. A fifteen-minute walk takes an hour if I don't keep him moving."

Jake knelt and rubbed the dog's head. "I like Fred. He's a real man's dog."

"Yeah, we love him. He's getting on in years. Daddy brought him home as a puppy about eight years ago."

The afternoon was gorgeous, not a dark cloud in the sky as the sun beat down on them. They laughed about the cold front that moved through and dropped the temps from the high to low nineties. There was a slight breeze as they strolled along the sidewalk.

Dressed for the summer heat, Lauren wore knee-length shorts with a sleeveless print blouse and sandals. Jake wore cargo shorts with a golf shirt and flip-flops. A cap bearing the embroidered Sleep Dreams logo hid his dark hair.

Homes gave way to the business district, and they passed a number of shops filled with tourists.

"There's the North Carolina Maritime Museum," Lauren told him. "They have classes and build boats."

Jake nodded. "You ever gone on the Ghost Walk?"

"No."

"I was reading about it last night. They go to Blackbeard's home?"

"Yes, Hammock House. It's the oldest house in Beaufort."

They strolled in silence for a while before Jake asked, "Aren't you charged by your first driving lesson? I remember feeling like I could take on the world after my first time."

She glanced at him. Obviously Jake thought she'd show more enthusiasm for their adventure. "Yeah. Sort of."

He stopped walking. "It's a beginning, Lauren. What other things did you want to do?"

She hesitated, wondering why she felt compelled to share facts about herself with him.

"Come on, tell me." Jake nudged her playfully. "Surely there's more you want to experience in life."

Could she even begin to list all the things she'd

considered? "Well, I'd like a place of my own," Lauren admitted. "A house. Not an apartment."

Jake nodded. "What else?"

"Maybe take more online college classes. And make some friends," she admitted shyly. "Mom and Dad are great, but I haven't had friends my age since I was diagnosed with narcolepsy."

"What happened to them?"

"I told you. It's too much for some people. Mom home-schooled me and we did some group things, but mostly it was just us."

He captured her hand. "Do you go anywhere to meet people?"

"Church and even there I keep to myself."

"Do the people at church know about your condition? Pray for you?"

"The pastor knows."

"What do you think people are going to do if you tell them the truth?"

She'd walked this path too many times not to know the answer. "They'll be afraid to hang out with me. I don't want to make people feel uncomfortable or have them making fun of me over something I can't control."

"You really worry that people will react negatively if you have an attack?"

She knew it to be a fact. She'd lived with this disorder long enough to know what reactions to expect. People might show genuine concern in the moment, but later when they recapped the experience, it became a joke. "I've met a few people online who have narcolepsy and we e-mail and chat. They understand."

"How does Ashleigh treat you?"

Yapper shot underneath Fred's leash. Lauren handed over the leash and moved to Jake's other side. He handed it back. "Like her boss. She's respectful and polite but keeps her distance."

Jake paused while Fred investigated a tree. "She wasn't happy that first day when she said I shouldn't be in your office. She called your dad. If Ashleigh didn't care, she'd have gone back to her desk and kept her mouth shut. Not risked getting me in trouble."

That didn't surprise her. "Could be she didn't want to get into trouble with Daddy. He made it clear that her job is to help me do my job." Lauren tugged the leash gently to bring Yapper back from her wandering. They passed two women who grinned at her and said, "Cute dog."

Lauren smiled back at them. "I like Ashleigh. She's a fun person. Keeps something going all the time. She volunteers and organizes lots of events at the office, and she's very popular with the other administrative staff. I often see them going to lunch together."

"How old are you? Twenty-five or so?"

"I turned twenty-seven on July first."

"Maybe you should suggest having lunch sometime. You're closer to her age. You have to give people a chance," Jake encouraged, "or you'll never find those you can trust."

"It's scary." She couldn't begin to explain how she dreaded activities outside the norm.

"I'm sure it is. Think about this, Lauren. If something happened to your parents, who would you depend on? You have to learn to be self-sufficient. They aren't doing you any favors with their coddling."

Offended, Lauren protested, "I do my part."

"I like your parents, but I think maybe they've protected you from too much."

In that instant, she wanted to tell Jake to mind his own business and stay out of her life. He couldn't begin to understand. "They do what they feel is best. You do the same for Teddy."

"Teddy's a baby," Jake said, coming to a halt. "That's something else. Why won't you hold him?"

Where had that question come from? Lauren flushed and glanced down at Yapper. "I don't know anything about children. I've never been around them."

"Kids adapt pretty quickly. If Teddy doesn't like something, he'll let you know."

She looked at him. "You should be afraid he could get hurt. Or left unsupervised if I had an attack. We need to head back. Mom expects us to help with dinner."

Upon realizing they were going home, Fred picked up his pace. Lauren considered what Jake had said. She'd watched movies and read books that gave her a glimpse of what other women experienced, not what she herself would feel. She prayed that God would send her someone to love, but as each day passed, it became more difficult to believe her knight in shining armor would ride into her world and make everything perfect.

In a very short time, Jake had pushed his way into her life and seemed to want her independence more than she did. He came off as a good friend who cared about her, but Lauren questioned his motivation. Why did Jake want her to be independent of her parents?

She opened the door and they stepped into the cool house.

Jake scooped up Yapper, disconnected the leash, and started to place her in the carrier.

"Don't do that." She took the little dog from him. Yapper lapped kisses of joy on Lauren's face. "We don't mind her running free."

"She'll irritate Fred. Besides, she's so tiny she could get hurt if someone doesn't realize she's there."

"Maybe he needs to be irritated. And she makes sure we know she's there. Do you have food?"

"In the car. I made a grocery store run earlier."

Lauren rolled her eyes. This man must spend his paycheck at the grocery. Seemed he shopped every day. "You should buy case lots. It would save you a fortune."

He flashed a wry smile. "Definitely cheaper than those late-night runs to the convenience store."

Lauren gasped. "You don't."

Sheepish, he admitted, "Sometimes. We run out of stuff. The convenience store is closer."

"You could use our membership at the wholesale club in Jacksonville. I'd be glad to go with you anytime. It's important to save money when you have a family."

"Thanks, Lauren. I might take you up on your offer."

"And thank you for what you did today," Lauren said.

"You did really well. I think we should get you a manual so you can study for your driving test. You can get a permit and once you're more comfortable driving on the highway, you could drive with your parents or a licensed adult."

"I found the manual online last night," she admitted.

They went into the kitchen, and her mother started issuing tasks like a drill sergeant. "Jake, the grill is hot. Throw those steaks on. Laurie, you can prepare the salad. Make that honey mustard dressing we like. I have potato wedges with olive oil and herbs roasting in the oven, and I prepared some of the corn we picked up over the weekend."

Her mother had fed Teddy, and now the baby played on a blanket in the family room.

Over dinner, they talked about her first driving experience and getting stuck in the sand. "She wanted to call you," Jake told Greg, "but we kept trying. You should have seen her. She handled it like a pro."

Greg glanced at his daughter. "Did you like driving?"

"For the most part. There was a time or two when I wasn't so sure."

There was reassurance in the smile her mother shared with her. "We've all been there. Learning to drive has its ups and downs, but it's quite an accomplishment once you master it."

Jake nodded and bit into an ear of corn. Afterward, he asked, "Did Lauren ever tell you she wants to fix up a little place of her own? A house?"

Suzanne looked dumbfounded. "No. Why haven't you told us this before?"

Lauren glared at Jake. Why had he done that?

"He asked about my life goals," she defended, emphasizing, "and it's a dream, a hope for one day. Not something I plan to rush out and do tomorrow."

"I suppose we could have converted the carriage house into an apartment for you," her mother said a couple of minutes later.

Lauren loved her bedroom. The large room had its own bath and closet with a window seat overlooking the waterfront. She'd spent hours curled up there, reading, watching television, listening to music, working on her laptop, even watching the waterfront.

"No." She glanced at Jake, giving him a silent *Look what you've done.* "I wondered what it would be like to have a place of my own. A small house where I could change the color or rearrange the furniture every week if I wanted."

Her dad harrumphed. "You obviously never painted. It's one of those less-is-better tasks. Right up there with rearranging furniture."

Lauren laughed. "You know what I mean, Daddy."

"You can repaint your room anytime you want."

She and her mother had redone the room a couple of years before. "It's fine, Mom. Really it is."

"What about one of the rental properties? There's that cute Victorian a couple of streets over. The tenants gave notice and will be moving by the end of September."

Lauren shook her head. "No. I wouldn't take advantage of you that way. If I thought I could manage, I'd have you find something I could afford."

"The house will be yours one day, Lauren. But if you prefer, you could pay rent. Let's see how you feel over the next few weeks and if things go well, your dad and I will help you paint the interior of the house any color you like."

She didn't know what to say. For years she'd fantasized about having her own place, thinking it an impossibility, and now all of a sudden everyone seemed to think it had become an achievable goal. Did she want to be alone when the attacks happened? It wasn't like having her own place would change anything. She would talk to her parents after Jake left. Make them understand her insecurities when it came to living on her own.

"Speaking of houses," Jake said to Suzanne, "Lauren showed me your parents' place today. I was wondering if you'd consider renting it short-term. I want to find a home and hire someone to stay with Teddy and Yapper while I work. You don't know anyone, do you?"

Suzanne nodded. "I might. A friend at church lost her job last year and hasn't been able to find anything. She's going stir-crazy and wants something to occupy her days. I could give you her number. You remember Mrs. Hart, don't you, Laurie?"

She remembered the woman well. Geraldine Hart had been her Sunday school teacher when she was a little girl. Lauren played with her daughter and stayed overnight in their home. Her friendship with Melissa Hart ended after Lauren's diagnosis. "She makes great cookies."

"I'll give her a call. So what about the house? We could live with it as it is."

Suzanne reached for her husband's plate and stacked it on top of her own. "I planned a few upgrades. I need to paint the kitchen and den and the porches and rockers. I'd also like to replace the appliances and tile the bathrooms."

"I could help with the renovation. I can paint," he added, sounding enthusiastic. "You buy the supplies and I'll provide the labor. I have some experience with tile, but you'd probably be better off with a professional."

"You've got a deal," Greg said quickly.

Suzanne laughed at her husband's eagerness to escape his most hated chore. "You're not getting off that easily. You can help."

"How much rental property do you have?" Jake asked.

"Five houses. I inherited my parents' place and two houses that belonged to my mother's aunts. I ran across the other two houses in the course of my work. As long as I keep the right tenants in place, they provide a good income. That's why I check references and require a security deposit."

Jake grinned broadly and said, "Well, you know where to find me. And we would take good care of the place. Yapper's housebroken, but I can restrict her to certain areas."

"Oh, don't do that," Suzanne said. "Mom and Dad had a dog. A retriever named Goldie. He slept in front of the fireplace." She chuckled and said, "If possible, he was lazier than Fred."

Lauren listened to their exchange as she chewed the final bite of her steak. It seemed her mother was giving the idea serious consideration. She doubted her mom could refuse Jake's hopeful expression.

"So you'll consider renting to me?"

"I need to do something with their things, but I don't see any reason you couldn't live there. In fact, I'll rent it fully furnished with the kitchen stuff and linens if you want."

"Perfect. We travel light. After Gwen died, I decided we didn't need the house. We moved what little furniture I kept into my uncle's loft apartment in New Mexico."

Lauren wanted to ask if he ever thought of settling down someplace but decided that was too personal. Obviously he'd eschewed the home his wife had made for their family in favor of practicality.

"I'll clean it out so you can move in next weekend," Suzanne said.

"Lauren mentioned that you were taking your time sorting through stuff," Jake began. "Teddy and I can live around anything you want to leave."

"That's sweet of you to offer, but there's a lot of stuff in the house that needs to go. I plan to donate their clothes to the church clothes closet. And they wanted Lauren to have their dining room table and china cabinet and the bedroom furniture. It's been in the family for generations."

"No sense putting it in storage when Jake can use it now," Lauren said.

Her mother nodded. "I'll pack up the china and Mama's bird collection. . ."

She choked up and Lauren quickly said, "I can do that. Daddy can take me over tomorrow after work."

"I'll take you," Jake said. "And I can use a broom or vacuum and dust. Let us handle this for you."

Lauren rested one hand on her mother's shoulder. "Yeah, Mom, we won't throw out anything."

"I'm their executrix, Laurie. I have to go through the papers and handle the legal stuff."

She remembered her mother doing the basic things required of the estate when her grandmother died. "I could box up everything and bring it here. I'll even organize it."

Her mother's warm smile encompassed them both. "I have to do it. I'll get started Tuesday."

Lauren glanced at her father. "Everything's under control at work. Okay if I help Mom?"

He nodded.

"Only if you have the time," Suzanne cautioned. "Don't get behind on my account."

Lauren glanced at Jake, wondering if he was going to object to her absence. He didn't say anything.

"We should have thought about you needing a place to stay before now," Suzanne said. "Living out of suitcases is a pain. I'd offer you Lauren's old crib, but I doubt it meets today's standards."

"Teddy had a nursery when Gwen was alive. The loft

apartment wasn't big enough for his furniture. I'll get a crib for the house."

"Are you okay with the other furnishings? There might be some pieces here if you wanted something different."

"Everything looked good to me," Jake said quickly. "I'm going to call your friend and see if she's interested in caring for Teddy and Yapper at the house. Thank you all. I can't tell you how much this helps."

"We're glad to have you with us," Greg told him as Suzanne served the chocolate silk pie she had made that afternoon.

five

"Sure you're up to this?" Lauren asked as her mother unlocked the door.

"Putting it off won't help. Plus, once we give Jake access, he'll do some of the work, which will save us money. I should let him stay rent free in exchange for his labor."

Lauren felt sad for her mom. She knew this would be difficult for her. "I don't think Jake would agree. Maybe you can charge him rent and no deposit instead."

"Maybe," her mother murmured thoughtfully.

"Where do we start?"

"We need to attack this room by room. I want Mom's china and bird collection out of the dining room. We'll leave the everyday stuff in the kitchen for Jake. Chuck those old pots and pans. You know how Mom was about holding on to everything."

"That new set is probably still in the box."

"They were expensive, too. Wonder what kind of cook Jake is? Maybe we should find him a cheaper set and you can take those for your place."

"Mom, I. . ." The urge to smack Jake grew stronger with each reference to her moving out. She hadn't gotten around to talking to them yet.

"I know, Laurie. It's not my intention to rush you, but we're willing to help if that's what you want. In fact, take anything of your grandmother's you'd like to have. We can put it in storage until you're ready."

"I'm in no hurry."

They moved systematically through the kitchen, sorting plasticware, recycled bags, dumping the junk drawer, sorting through the dish towels and other items.

"I never understood why Mom didn't toss this stuff," Suzanne said. "She had better."

Lauren shrugged. "I'm sure she planned to bleach out the stains, and you know everything in the junk drawer always has a purpose."

Her mother opened the cabinet and loaded the dishes into the dishwasher. She ripped the paper from the emptied shelf and tossed it toward the trash can. "We need new shelf liner. This hasn't been replaced recently."

Then she removed a handful of mismatched stainless silverware from the drawer. "I think this will be okay. Mom's silver chest is in the dining room. Don't let me forget that." The utensils clinked as she dropped them into the silverware basket.

They wrapped items in bubble wrap and pulled pieces of furniture into the living room to be moved into storage.

"I should take the file cabinet."

"What about the boxes in the attic?" Lauren asked. "They kept every financial document they've ever had."

"I'll check, but we can get a shredding company to handle those. I don't need to keep everything."

"There's no telling what's hidden in this house. She might have a fortune hidden up there. You know how Gram was about keeping money everywhere."

Suzanne patted her jeans pocket. "I'm several dollars richer."

"Me, too," Lauren declared.

"Let's see who collects the most."

"You're on."

Her mother sighed. "I don't think this is going to be a one-day task."

The keep, toss, and donate boxes turned into piles as they pulled out the elderly couple's treasures. When they filled the last of the boxes they'd bought, her mother said, "I'll call your dad to bring more."

Greg Kingsley arrived around noon bringing lunch, boxes, and Jake. "We're here to help."

"You could haul that pile to the dump."

Her father's eyebrows rose. "What do you plan to do with the rest of it?"

Suzanne shrugged. "Storage, I suppose."

"Hey, Mom, check this out." Lauren climbed down the stairs from the attic and drew to a halt at the sight of Jake.

Self-consciously, she brushed back the hair that had come loose from her braid and brushed at the jeans shorts and T-shirt that were smudged with dust. "Hi. I didn't realize you were here."

"I came to help."

"Who's running the plant?"

Greg chuckled. "Same people who do it every day. They know where to find us."

"What did you find, Laurie?" her mother asked.

She handed over a stack of towels. "There are trunks of new stuff up there."

Greg looked at his wife. "We can't keep everything, Suzanne."

"I don't plan to. Laurie will take anything she wants, and we'll leave some for Jake's use, and the rest will be donated." She waved toward the piles. "You can see we've been sorting and tossing, but the attic's full to overflowing. There's a lifetime of memories up there."

"You could install a lock on the attic door and leave it for now," Jake suggested.

"A lock?"

Lauren noted her mother's curious look.

He shrugged. "I thought you'd feel more comfortable knowing it was secure."

"I trust you, Jake. I wouldn't let you live here otherwise."

Jake nodded. "Better to take your time. You're always hearing about the finds people make because someone didn't know they had a treasure. I spoke with Mrs. Hart, and we're going to see how Teddy responds to her."

Suzanne piled the towels on the table. "Will she cook and clean?"

Jake shook his head. "I didn't include that in the job description. I need someone to make sure Teddy's safe and to keep Yapper out of trouble. I can handle the chores."

"I'm sure Gerry wouldn't mind," Suzanne said. "She could put something in the Crock-Pot or stick a casserole in the oven."

"We'll see. If Teddy likes her, I don't want to risk running her off."

They continued the conversation over lunch at the kitchen table.

"Hey, Jake, let's haul this trash to the plant Dumpsters."

The screen door banged behind them, and the women returned to their tasks.

"Trash is gone," Jake told Lauren when he walked into the living room later. "What else can I do?"

"Sort through those magazines," she said, indicating piles underneath the end tables and in a magazine rack. Lauren handed him a pair of scissors. "Remove the address labels. We'll donate them to the hospital."

He set to work and soon had the magazines sorted. "There's some mail I found. And this."

Jake held the birthday card she'd given her grandmother, a fifty sticking out of the envelope.

"She looked for this everywhere," Lauren said, a sad smile on her face.

Her parents came down from the attic, and her mom dropped onto the sofa. Her face was pink with her exertion.

"Look what Jake found in the magazines." She held up the card.

"She felt so bad about losing your present."

"I'll donate it to the church in her name."

"Good idea." Suzanne swiped at a tear that trailed along her cheek.

Greg reached for her hand. "You're not doing this too soon, are you, Suze?"

"No, sweetie. I'm fine."

The washer buzzer went off.

Her mother stood. "That's the towels. I'll hang them on the clothesline. They smell so much fresher when air-dried."

"I'll do it," Lauren offered.

"No. Keep sorting. I need fresh air."

Lauren went back to the books. She found a photo of her very young grandparents tucked inside one and studied it closely. They had been so in love. Marriage longevity was a given in her family. "Until death do us part" had been the case with both sets of grandparents, and her parents had recently celebrated their thirtieth anniversary.

"Who do you have there?" Jake leaned down to take a look.

"My grandparents."

"Nice-looking couple."

"They'd been married over fifty years when Grandpa died."

She laid the picture aside. If her mom didn't want it, she'd keep it for herself. Or maybe she could put a collection of photos into a digital frame for her mom's birthday.

Her parents left to take a load to the charity resale shop. Lauren and Jake continued working, and by late afternoon they had sorted through the items in the living room. Lauren went outside to collect the towels, and Jake followed. He lifted them to his face and breathed deeply. "They smell like sunshine."

"Could be the fabric softener," Lauren teased.

He folded the towel and laid it in the basket. "Nah. Too fresh. Your mom doesn't need to do all this stuff. She's got enough to do already."

"Mom's a homemaker at heart. She'll do everything she can before you move in."

She reached for another towel. "I meant to tell you, there are lots of toys in the attic. You might want to check them out for Teddy."

"Yours?"

She nodded. "I was the only grandchild."

"He might break them."

"It's okay, Jake. I don't mind sharing my toys."

He carried the basket into the laundry room. The Kingsleys entered a few minutes later.

"I need to pick up Teddy and Yapper. I can get pizza and salad for dinner if you want to keep working."

"Let's stop for the day," Suzanne said. "We've made good progress."

Jake appeared bothered by the situation. "I feel I'm pushing you. I can find another place."

"Don't. Mom would be happy knowing you and Teddy will be living here. You have plenty of household stuff, and the new fridge and stove will be delivered tomorrow. Once you buy groceries and we pick up shelf paper, you'll be in business."

"I can do that," Jake said.

Suzanne nodded. "Greg's going to have them bring over a new mattress. You need to decide which one you want."

"It's not necessary," Jake objected.

"Ah, but a Sleep Dreams mattress makes you a better employee," Suzanne teased.

"I'd have to write a testimonial."

Lauren grinned broadly as she set four bottles of water on the table. "And then you can star in the commercial."

Jake opened his and chugged half the bottle. "You don't think people will feel I'm paid for my opinion?"

"No more so than they'll think we are. Hey, we could put Teddy in a crib and let him cry, and then put him on a Sleep Dreams bed and watch him go off to sleep right away. Sales for new parents would skyrocket."

"Or parents might be discouraged if they thought their kids would have to sleep with them. Maybe you should develop a crib mattress line."

"Never thought about that," Greg said.

"Do you purchase booths at the home shows? I've been meaning to ask."

"We haven't."

"Might want to check into it this year." Jake glanced at his watch and frowned. "I need to go. See you tomorrow."

She watched him walk out the front door and climb into his vehicle. Lauren didn't doubt Jake would have worked into the night if they had been willing. He was certainly eager to get out of the hotel.

six

Sleep eluded Lauren as her mind filled with all she'd done that day. After their fast-food dinner, she showered and lay in bed thinking of the time she'd spent with Jake.

Was today an example of what it would be like to create a home for a husband and family? A time or two she had fantasized that they were setting up their own home, choosing the bits and pieces that would surround them.

When had she started thinking of Jake like that? Just because he'd been nice to her didn't mean he had any interest beyond that of work. Sure, he'd encouraged her to make friends, but somehow she didn't think that included her falling for him.

The next morning she dressed and went to the office with her father. They discussed the day on their drive in and decided Lauren would go back out to the farm after handling a couple of things that needed doing.

She read her e-mail, returned a few phone calls, and gave Ashleigh a to-do list. Lauren called her dad to say she was ready. "Let's pick up lunch on the way," she suggested.

They met Jake coming up the hall.

"I was on my way to see you," he told Greg.

"Let me run Lauren out to help her mother. I'll be back within the hour."

"Give me a call." Jake glanced at Lauren. "Back to the sorting, huh?"

She nodded. "Mom's determined, and we don't want her doing it alone."

Jake's chest heaved with his mighty sigh. "I hate putting this extra stress on her."

Lauren's head tilted in her dad's direction. "Mom's not stressed. He's trying to figure out what to do with the stuff she's bringing home."

"House was already full to overflowing," he muttered.

Her father would be labeled a minimalist. He hated clutter and while her mother tried to please him, she insisted she needed a certain amount of frills in her life.

Lauren squeezed his arm. "Don't worry. We'll get it all put away."

"I'll come over later and help," Jake volunteered.

"I'm sure there will be plenty to do."

"And I'm taking a delivery truck over tonight," Greg said. "Why don't you choose a mattress, and I'll take it when I go."

"You don't have to do that," Jake objected.

Lauren wanted to laugh. He was getting a firsthand view of her parents' generosity.

Greg clapped him on the back. "Sure we do."

They arrived to find her mother had washed the curtains and they fluttered in the slight breeze.

"Here you go." Lauren passed her the food bag. "We ate ours on the way over. What's on today's agenda?"

"Mom's bedroom."

Lauren groaned. "Did we save the worst for last?"

"Probably. I bought more boxes. We're donating her things, but I thought maybe I'd offer a few of her nicer pieces to Miss Bessie."

Bessie Shaw had been her grandmother's best friend.

Lauren nodded. "Go put your feet up and eat your lunch. I'll get started."

In the bedroom, she looked at the line of boxes her mother had hauled into the room and knew they would need them. Gram loved clothes.

She tugged on the pulls for the first drawer and wasn't surprised when her action met resistance. Lauren used one hand to push down the contents and the other to pull the drawer from the dresser. Settling it on the bed, she picked up the first piece. Clean but shabby. She shoved it into a trash bag.

Lauren couldn't bring herself to discard the pieces Gram had worn often. As she stroked the colorful shirt, she decided to ask the ladies at church to make a memory quilt for her mother.

There were rolls of dollar bills and containers of pennies tucked into the drawer. Lauren smiled. This new haul would push her over the top in their competition. She assumed the plastic flower in the squashed gift box had some sort of sentimental meaning along with the empty body powder container. "Sorry, Gram," she whispered as she slipped them into the trash.

She had emptied three drawers by the time her mother came into the room. Suzanne pulled out another.

"Jake's really concerned that he's stressing you with all this."

"He's sensitive because he's gone through the same thing recently. I should consider this a lesson not to put you through this when I go."

Lauren never wanted to consider life without her parents. "Daddy's not happy. You know how he is about clutter."

Her mother folded clothes and tucked them into the donation box. "He doesn't have a lot of stuff from his parents' estate. They disposed of most of their possessions when they went into assisted living. Letting go is difficult. I know I'll do a more extensive disposal after I've had time to work through the loss, but for now I'm keeping what needs to be kept. I went through her Christmas decorations this morning." She smiled at Lauren. They shared a love of all things Christmas. "I kept the things you made for her."

Lauren looked up from her sorting. "You didn't keep those paper cups wrapped in aluminum foil, did you?"

Suzanne nodded. "Her joy bells. They're precious, Laurie."

"Promise they won't end up on our tree at home."

She shook her head. "Can't do that."

They were both thinking memories. "Okay, Mom. Whatever you want."

They soon had the dresser and chest emptied. Lauren opened the closet door and looked at her mother. It was packed tight. They pulled blankets and old purses from the top shelf, jumping back when things Gram had hidden underneath clattered to the floor.

Suzanne pulled a handful of papers from the first purse. "We'll have to go through these."

Lauren picked up a small box and set it on the bed. "Secondary filing system?" They laughed and dumped the papers inside, adding the handbags to the growing donation pile.

Later they surveyed the boxes and bags.

"Gram will help a lot of people today," Lauren said.

"What about those?" Her mother indicated the pile of older pieces on the bed.

Lauren quickly swept the clothes she'd reserved into a bag. "Let's get this stuff out to the porch."

Her mother dragged a plastic bag toward the door. Lauren waited until she was out of sight before shoving the keeper bag into a dresser drawer.

They had loaded the last box in her mother's car when her father arrived. Greg kissed his wife and said, "Jake will be over as soon as he picks up Teddy and Yapper."

"Ride to the church with me. Lauren can wait for them." She glanced at her daughter. "The bedroom could do with a dust and vacuum."

They had already lugged out the old mattress and dismantled the double bed that matched her grandmother's antique furniture in preparation for the new king-sized bed. "I'll take care of it."

And then she'd hide those clothes in one of the boxes she planned to take home with her.

❧

Jake unbuckled Teddy's car seat and removed him from the vehicle. He reached for the pet carrier and placed Yapper in the shade on the porch. The screen door bounced slightly with his tap.

A vacuum roared to life, and he doubted anyone could hear him over the noise. He glanced at his son. "What do you think, Teddy? Should we let ourselves in?"

It occurred to him that their unannounced presence might frighten whoever was inside.

"Come on, buddy, we'll wait here in the swing."

Jake slipped off his sport coat and rolled up his shirt-sleeves. He couldn't get over the feeling that he'd come home. They were going to be happy here in the country. He filled Yapper's water bottle at the outside faucet and returned it to the bag before settling in the swing.

The vacuum shut off, but before he could announce his presence, Lauren came out of the house with a couple of throw rugs.

"Hi."

As feared, she screamed and the rugs went flying. "Sorry." Jake stood and picked up his son.

Lauren rested a hand against her chest. "I didn't know you were here."

"Only five minutes or so. Didn't want to scare you."

"Too late for that." She bent to pick up the rugs. "We finished downstairs. You can move in any time you like."

Jake's gaze widened. These Kingsley women were something else. "You mean like now?"

"The curtains need to be ironed and rehung and your new mattress brought inside."

"Would you watch Teddy while I run to the hotel for our things?"

Lauren all but cringed, and Jake knew she was afraid to be left alone with his son.

"Mom will be back soon. Could you go then?"

"Yeah. Maybe it's best to move in tomorrow." He pointed to the truck. "Do you have the key? I'll bring the new mattress inside."

"You can't move it alone," she protested. "Mom and I had a time getting the other set out."

"I'll back the truck closer."

She shrugged. "The keys are on the counter."

"Here, take Teddy."

She held the grinning baby tightly when his father charged into the house. "Your dad doesn't take no for an answer, does he?"

"I heard that," Jake yelled from inside.

Teddy blew a spit bubble in response.

"Got 'em," Jake said, jangling the keys as he ran down the steps. "Yell when I get close enough to pull the ramp out."

She called out when he neared the porch steps. He jumped out and came around to roll up the truck door and slide the ramp from underneath onto the porch.

Lauren glanced at Teddy. "How do I maneuver a mattress and hold him at the same time?"

Taking his son, Jake went inside and settled him on the carpeted floor with a couple of toys.

"Will he stay there?" While he wasn't exactly crawling, she'd seen Teddy scoot about on his bottom.

"Yeah. For a few minutes. Let's do this before he starts crying."

Lauren lifted one end of the first twin box spring that would serve as a foundation for the new king mattress. The screen door creaked as they entered and worked their way toward the bedroom.

After they finished doing the same with the second box spring, the mattress proved unwieldy and it shoved Lauren back against the side of the truck when Jake picked up his end. "Hey, watch it," she called in protest.

"Sorry." Together they carried it into the living room.

"Jake, look," Lauren said at the sight of Teddy holding on to the sofa.

"That's a new trick he's picked up recently. Mom said I walked early."

"You need to childproof that hearth. Once he starts walking, he could fall and hit his head."

"Let's put this in the bedroom, and I'll come back for him."

They leaned it against the dresser. "Whew," Lauren declared, blowing her bangs out of her face. "That's one heavy mattress."

"Made to last. I need sheets."

She pointed to the top of the chest of drawers where a set of crisp, clean white sheets waited. "Mom brought over a new set she had at the house. She even washed them for you."

"Air-dried, too?"

"Of course. Mom insists everything needs to be aired out. She even opened the windows and doors and refused to run the air conditioner for a while today. Do you know how hot it was?"

He shook his head in wonder at the Kingsleys' generosity. They seemed determined to do everything possible to set him up for housekeeping.

"Let me grab Teddy, and you can hold on to him while I put my bed together."

He returned to find Lauren pulling the bed frame from the cardboard box he'd brought in earlier. Jake took over as she took Teddy and lounged in her grandmother's comfortable armchair.

Once he had the frame assembled, she placed Teddy on the carpeted floor and helped Jake slide the box springs and mattress into place. Lauren dropped the fitted mattress cover on the bed. "Mom had this, too. It's waterproof, which will be a plus if you plan to sleep with Teddy."

They stood on opposite sides working together to make

the bed. Once the fitted sheet was in place, Jake flapped the top sheet, laughing each time it fluttered from Lauren's grasp.

Exasperated by his play, she grabbed the sheet and jerked it down onto the bed, tucking the edges underneath the mattress. Jake fell backward across the bed and lay spread-eagled. She stared and he saw her cheeks flush.

"Pillows." She hurried off to find them.

Teddy cried out in protest, and Jake rolled off. He scooped him up and bounced him on the mattress. "What do you think, buddy? You like our new bed?"

The baby jabbered. Lauren returned. "Here they are."

She slipped cases on the pillows and placed them at the head of the bed. "Mom found a bedspread at home and took it to the dry cleaners. You have clean towels and washcloths in the bathroom and dish towels in the kitchen."

"I got the shelf liner last night."

"You want to start on that?"

He smiled at her and shook his head. "Not right this minute." Jake picked Teddy up and headed for the living room. There he sat in an armchair, holding the baby in his lap. "I can't tell you how much I appreciate this. This house and a yard will make a big difference for Teddy and Yapper."

Lauren and her parents had become very important to him in a short time. His first impression of Lauren had been so off base. She deserved so much more out of life than she had gotten.

After a few minutes, he handed Teddy over and said, "Show me the boxes. I'll start loading them, and we can decide what to do about dinner when your parents get back."

She pointed to the stacks over by the built-in bookcases. "Those are books." She indicated the half dozen or so marked "fragile". "These have breakable things."

"Better not pack them underneath the books," Jake teased.

She smiled back. "No, let's not."

"You watch my little man, and I'll load your boxes without

breaking anything." Lauren nodded agreement, and he sat Teddy on the floor with a small collection of his toys. She picked up an old wooden block she'd told him she'd played with and handed it to the baby. Jake watched for a while as Teddy dropped it and waited for her to hand it back. He was very familiar with this game.

Jake walked out to the porch to retrieve the cart. Back inside, he loaded the first box of books. He wheeled it into the truck and returned to the living room.

As he moved through the room, Jake glanced over and stopped suddenly when he saw Lauren sprawled on the floor next to the end table. He moved quickly, calling her name. Teddy sat close to her, patting her arm and calling, "*Lalalala.*"

Blood oozed from her forehead. She must have hit her head when she fell. Panicked, he grabbed a tissue box from the table and pulled out a handful. He dabbed at the area, thankful when he found it to be more of a scratch.

Jake did what he could to make her more comfortable and sat there with her and Teddy, waiting for Lauren to wake. He wanted to shake her, see those hazel eyes, and know she would be okay. It worried him that he hadn't been there for her when she needed him.

A few minutes later, Lauren came awake, looking at him in surprise.

"Does your head hurt? Can you hold this while I get a bandage? You're bleeding."

"Bleeding?"

He shrugged. "You were sitting on the sofa when I went out. I found you here."

"Teddy decided to practice his throwing arm. He bounced a block off the end table. I suppose I had an attack when I stood up to get it. How long?"

"A few minutes."

Their gazes met, and she saw the concern in his eyes as he looked down at her. Emotion swelled in Lauren when she realized Jake hadn't run away from the situation.

"Help me up?" she implored.

He took her hands and pulled her to her feet. "Does your head hurt? I don't think you need stitches. It's more of a scratch." Jake didn't let go as he helped her over to the sofa. He glanced back to make sure Teddy was close by.

His touch was comforting, almost tempting Lauren to cling.

"Here, hold these," he said, placing her hand over the tissues. He took Teddy and went into the bathroom to search for first-aid supplies. He returned with a thumb bandage and gauze. "This was all I could find."

He pulled the backing off, his fingers gentle as he probed the area and then affixed the small piece of gauze with the bandage. "Not bad," he murmured. "You think we need ice?"

She shook her head. "I'll be okay."

Her parents returned and everything reverted to normal. Her father and Jake carried out boxes while her mother took the bedspread she'd picked up from the dry cleaners into the bedroom and came back. "You two have been busy." Her expression looked puzzled. "What's that on your forehead?"

"All Jake could find in the way of first aid. I fell and hit my head on the end table."

Her mother's gaze fixed on her. "Everything okay?"

Lauren nodded. "Just a scratch. I hoped. . . The last couple of days. . ."

Her mother knew what she was trying to say. "You've been pretty active."

Activity did help stave off the attacks, but not today. She shrugged. "I hope Jake understands the danger in leaving Teddy alone with me."

"Laurie. . ."

"Please, Mom. I know what you're going to say. It never changes. We all have to accept that."

"No," Suzanne declared with a shake of her head. "Every

day without an attack is a good day. You've been attack-free for longer periods lately. That's wonderful."

For Lauren, wonderful would be never having another sleep attack.

Jake and her dad came back inside.

"I'd like to take everyone out tonight."

Suzanne flashed Jake an apologetic smile. "I'm sorry. We invited Pastor and Mrs. Bell to dinner. It's their anniversary. Laurie could go with you."

She mumbled, "I need to go home."

The elephant was back in the room, and Lauren didn't want to deal with him.

"I wish you'd stay," Jake said simply.

She pinned him with a serious stare. "So you can babysit me while Mom and Dad are away? I've been alone after attacks before."

The dark brows slanted in a frown, an edge to his voice when he said, "You shouldn't let these attacks get you down."

She glared at him. "Don't you think I know that?" Lauren tried to accept her lot in life and live with the complications of her condition. There were many—depression, difficulty in concentrating, extreme exhaustion, increased irritability, and the list went on. Then Jake Greer had come along, and she'd somehow gotten it in her head that maybe she could be normal for a change.

"Come on, Laurie," he pleaded, using her parents' name for her. "Join us for dinner. We want you to stay, don't we, buddy?"

As if to voice his agreement, Teddy looked over from where he had pulled himself up on a chair, grinned, and bounced up and down.

"Say yes, Lauren," he pleaded, a strange, faintly eager look in the blue-green gaze.

She wanted to. Why not? No sense in going home and sitting alone, moaning and groaning about her pitiful life. "Okay."

"I'll bring her home," Jake said.

"We won't be late," Lauren said. "Jake can't keep Teddy out past his bedtime."

"We could run by and pick you up after dinner," Greg suggested.

"That would be even better."

"Are you staying here tonight?" Suzanne asked Jake.

"I thought maybe we'd run by the hotel." He glanced at Lauren and said, "If you're okay with that?"

"Sure."

After they left, Jake changed Teddy and carried him out to the car. He gave the baby a bottle. Teddy leaned back in the car seat, sucking down the formula with obvious enjoyment.

He started the vehicle and said, "Oh man, I forgot Yapper."

"Done," he said as he climbed back in the car minutes later. Teddy had fallen asleep. "I walked Yapper and set her up in the bathroom. If she has an accident, she won't hurt the tile floor."

Jake drove over to the hotel, parked, and looked at Lauren. "Let's check to see if you're still bleeding." His fingers were gentle against her forehead as he peeled the bandage free. "It's stopped. I'll take it off so people don't look at you funny. I have a little first-aid kit in the room if it starts back."

They took a luggage cart up to the room where he and Teddy had been living. "I started packing last night. We've amassed a lot of stuff in a very short time."

Jake laid Teddy in the crib and picked up two boxes. He set one on the small kitchen counter. "If you pack this stuff, I'll take care of the bathroom."

Lauren admired the neat array in the small cabinet space. Jake had organized their instant food packets in plastic bins. She placed them in the cardboard box.

"That's it for the bathroom." He glanced around once more and flipped off the light.

He carried a shaving kit and the box contained very little.

"Can I put some stuff in that box?"

Jake pulled out a drawer and used a plastic bag for the items. Handing it over, he opened the small fridge and loaded the items into a cooler while she finished up. Then he stacked the cooler, boxes, and his luggage on the cart.

"Can you carry Teddy down to the car?"

Lauren shook her head. No way. He could be hurt if she had an attack and fell. "I can steer the luggage cart into the elevator."

Lauren watched his attempt to analyze her fear. He'd never witnessed her drop during an attack. Had no idea what could happen if she did.

"I'll do it. Will you stay here with Teddy?"

Apprehension filled her as Lauren recalled her earlier failure. She didn't want to disappoint him.

"Are you afraid you'll have another attack?"

She nodded.

"It won't take long to unload this stuff. I'll stop by the desk and come back."

Teddy woke while Jake was gone. Lauren tried to console him as he cried and called for his dad.

"He'll be right back," she said softly, jiggling the baby in hopes of calming him. She looked around and spotted the colorful fabric toy tucked under the pillow. "Here's your truck." She rolled the stuffed vehicle over his legs and up his chest.

He took the toy and pounded it up and down on the bed.

Lauren bounced playfully and said, "Rough ride, huh, Teddy?"

The baby grinned.

She glanced up to find Jake watching from the doorway. "Here's your daddy," she declared, sounding more relieved than she intended. Teddy all but threw himself from the bed.

"*Dadadada.*"

"Words to steal a man's heart," he murmured, swinging his

son into the air. "Ready?"

He tossed the keycard on the desk along with a tip for the housekeeper. Jake held the door as Lauren gave the room a final search and picked up a couple of toys that had fallen off the bed.

"What are your plans for tomorrow?" Jake asked as they walked down the hallway.

"The usual. Laundry and chores around the house."

"You have time to go crib-hunting with us?"

Surprised, she said, "I don't know anything about cribs."

"I thought maybe we could work out the mystery with the help of a sales clerk."

She hit the DOWN button for the elevator. "Let's ask Mom. Maybe she knows someone who has one you can borrow."

The door slid open. "Okay. Feel up to a grocery store run?"

Lauren had never pushed herself after an attack. She generally took it easy but not tonight. She stepped into the elevator. "Sure."

They drove to the nearest grocery store. Jake parked and got out, taking Teddy from his seat. "This isn't our favorite chore," he said as they walked toward the store.

"I don't know many people who enjoy grocery shopping."

Jake pulled out a cart and settled Teddy in the seat.

"You need to wipe those things down," Lauren declared. "They have so many bacteria."

"Mom says a little dirt never hurt anyone."

"Let's not test that theory." She pulled wipes from the canister next to the door and cleaned the cart handle. Teddy rewarded her effort by grabbing the stainless steel bar.

In the produce section, Jake bagged items. She noted he chose one or two of some fruits but opted for a big bundle of bananas. "Our favorite."

He bought staple items along with baby food and diapers. They checked out.

"Ouch," she said when the cashier announced his total.

He grimaced and pushed the cart toward the door. Lauren helped unload the groceries into the trunk.

Back at the house, they reversed the process. While Jake set up the small grill he'd purchased, Lauren unpacked the perishables and formed the hamburger into patties. Teddy sat on the kitchen floor. Good thing her mom insisted on mopping it earlier in the week.

Jake came in from the deck and washed his hands. "Charcoal's on."

He opened the fridge and removed a packet of hot dogs. "You want a dog and a burger?"

Lauren shook her head. "A hamburger is plenty. Are we having chips?"

Jake nodded. "And lettuce, tomato, cheese, and pickles on our burgers. I'm a ketchup and mustard fan. What about you?"

"Me, too."

He dropped two hot dogs on the plate with the burgers and rummaged around until he found the seasoning he'd purchased along with a bottle of steak sauce, a small bowl, and a basting brush.

Jake sorted through the baby food and picked up two jars. He reached for Teddy. "I suppose a high chair would be another worthwhile purchase."

Lauren rinsed her hands and dried them with a paper towel. "There's one in the attic. Why don't you get it while the charcoal heats up?"

The wooden chair had been in the family for years. Lauren sprayed antibacterial cleaner liberally and wiped it down with a clean cloth. "There, good as new."

"Let's see how he likes it." Jake placed Teddy in the chair and pulled the wooden tray over his head. "What do you think, buddy?"

Lauren used a damp cloth to wipe the baby's hands. Teddy pounded boisterously as Jake sliced a banana onto a paper plate. The baby attacked the small bits.

"Be right back. I need to check the grill."

Lauren heated the baby food and picked up the small spoon. "Hey, Teddy, let's say grace." She whispered, "God is good, God is great, and we thank Him for our food. By God's hand we must be fed, give us Lord, our daily bread. Amen."

Teddy pounded the tray.

She took a little food on the spoon, and Teddy consumed it almost faster than she could shovel it into his mouth.

"He was hungry," she said when Jake returned.

Jake seasoned the burgers and picked up the plate. "If you finish feeding him, I'll get these started." She nodded and he disappeared out the back door.

Lauren felt she'd accomplished a major task when she wiped Teddy's hands and face after his meal. She pushed the screen door open and asked, "Did you want to get him ready for bed?"

He glanced up from flipping the burgers. Flames shot up, and Jake used a spray bottle to knock them back. "I take him into the shower with me in the morning."

"He takes showers?" she asked curiously. How did Jake manage a shower with a baby in his arms?

"Yeah. He likes them."

"He'd probably love a tub bath more," Lauren said.

"We'll have to give it a try. Did you give him a bottle?"

"Not yet." She started back inside and paused. "Did you feed Yapper?"

He grunted. "Not yet."

"I'll get her."

Lauren opened the door, and the tiny dog raced into the kitchen, barking and joyous over her escape.

"Cut that out or I'll put you back," Jake commanded when he came in for a clean plate.

"It's just her way of letting you know where she is. Where's her bowl?"

"Bathroom. I gave her water before we left."

She retrieved the dishes and filled them with fresh water and food. Yapper ate almost as greedily as Teddy. She supposed it was later than their usual mealtimes.

Jake toasted the buns on the grill and brought the food into the kitchen. They sat at the kitchen table. Jake said grace and stacked his burger so high Lauren wondered how he would get it into his mouth. He did so without difficulty. She shook her head in disbelief.

Much later, after they consumed what Lauren thought might have been the best burger she'd ever eaten, and Teddy was asleep and Yapper had settled down, they sat contented and happy.

"You want dessert? I bought ice cream."

"Maybe later," Lauren said, so stuffed she doubted she could eat another bite.

Jake stretched out his legs before him and laid his hands over his stomach. "I like this house. Feels like home."

Lauren noted his new air of contentment. "It does. Gram always said it had a lot of heart. Gramps offered to build her something bigger and she refused. Said this house was perfect as far as she was concerned. She let him make improvements, like redoing the kitchen and bathrooms and replacing carpet and flooring, but the rest stayed the same. They were happy here.

"Gram missed Gramps. We tried to get her to move in with us, but she didn't want to leave her home. I offered to stay here, but she said she'd be okay and she was. After she got sick, Mom stayed most nights."

"It would have been hard for her to leave."

Lauren nodded.

"Are you feeling better?"

As his gaze swept over her face, Lauren felt embarrassed. "I'm good. Sorry I snapped at you, but I get frustrated."

"You're entitled."

She shook her head. "No, I'm not. It's not your fault. And

my situation could be worse."

Jake's gaze rested on her. "You said your mom home-schooled you?"

She nodded. "She handled the company finances at the time and took me to work with her. She would work with me on my assignments and then leave me to read or do my math problems."

"Why didn't you stay in school?"

"The system wasn't equipped to handle my condition. Mom insisted I was intelligent and capable of learning. She didn't want me labeled because of my problem. I didn't graduate with my class, but I finished school about the same time. Mom trained me to take over the job. She wanted to get back into real estate."

"Where was your dad in all this?"

"Running the company. Teaching me what he could. They're great parents. At times I feel I've destroyed their lives, but they never complain."

"They love you," he said simply. "Nothing can change that."

"I resent burdening them. I follow my routine faithfully and then when the attacks happen, I'm disappointed because it failed. I pray all the time that God will relieve me of this thorn in my side, but it's never gone away."

"Did you want to become the company CFO?"

She had thought about what she would have done with her life if she'd been normal. "I wanted to support myself, and this was a job I could handle."

"You're afraid to go after your dreams."

She let out a choked, almost desperate laugh. "It's not the dreams that make me afraid. It's the reality. What if I fall and hit my head? Or I'm cooking and have an attack? Or if I drive and cause an accident? If someone gets hurt or even killed, how do I live with that?"

Jake shrugged. "But what if none of that happens?"

Lauren didn't have an answer.

Their gazes met and held. "We all have to accept our lot in life. I never imagined I'd become a single dad. Most mornings I don't think I'll get Teddy and Yapper out of the house, but I do." He held up his hand and admitted, "I know mothers do it every day. But I had no experience."

She used a paper napkin to wipe the moisture from her glass. "Have you considered that you will have to settle down when Teddy starts school? Kids need stability. I don't see that happening with him in a new place every few months."

"You live with what you know. If that's the life Teddy lives, he'll adapt."

"What about marriage? More kids? Have you completely ruled out the possibility?" Lauren wanted to hear Jake's answer to that.

"No. Not at all. If the right woman comes into our lives, we'll adapt, too."

"Adapt?" Lauren considered that a strange response.

"Sure. Couples adapt in marriage or it doesn't last. Gwen and I had our problems because we couldn't. I suppose I sound like a jerk for admitting that."

Lauren shrugged. "I can't judge you. Only you know what went on between you and your wife."

"Our family and friends considered me selfish for refusing to give up the job I loved to come home and be a full-time husband and father."

"Like people consider me selfish because I still live with my parents?"

He frowned. "But you're justified in what you do."

"They don't know why I live my cowardly existence. I'm sure there's more than one person who wonders why I live in my parents' home instead of living my own life."

There was a flash of lights as her parents' car pulled into the driveway. She glanced at the kitchen clock, surprised to find it was after nine. "My ride's here," she said unnecessarily.

"You're not a coward, Laurie," Jake said. "Thanks for joining me for dinner tonight. I've enjoyed it."

Lauren picked up her purse from the end table. "Me, too. I'll ask Mom about the crib. Thanks for dinner, Jake. Sleep well."

"On my new mattress?"

They laughed and he reached for her hand. "Thanks, Lauren. You and Suzanne worked so hard to make this happen. I owe you."

"You do. Take care of Gram's house for us. And be happy."

He kissed her cheek. "I'll talk to you tomorrow."

Jake pulled open the door for her, and Lauren walked onto the porch, raising a hand in greeting to her parents. He followed and did the same.

She climbed into the backseat of her father's car. Her mother looked back at her. "Are they all settled in?"

"Getting there."

Suzanne smiled at her daughter.

seven

Jake showered and made his way into the bedroom. He removed the pillow bumpers and settled next to his son who sprawled contentedly in the middle of the bed. Comfortable, he thought as the mattress conformed to the contours of his body.

He owed the Kingsleys for making this house work for him and Teddy. Jake planned on renting an apartment, but that day when he'd come here with Lauren, the place called out to him. She was right about one thing—it was a home. He didn't blame her grandmother for not wanting it changed. The house was perfect.

Yapper came to the bedside and barked. "Go get in your bed," he ordered softly.

After Yapper settled down, Jake thought about how upset Lauren had been over her attack.

Jake considered what Lauren had told him about her fear of reality. He'd never meant to stress her with his suggestions. Why had he come on so strong in encouraging Lauren to strike out on her own? He'd pushed the lesson immediately when she voiced a desire to drive and even brought up the subject of a house to her parents. That had upset Lauren. Jake knew he shouldn't have done it, but it seemed right at the time.

He liked Lauren. He wouldn't deny her condition frightened him. He couldn't help but see her as another needy female. Was that why he'd pushed so hard for her to become more independent?

Surely not, he thought, giving himself the benefit of the doubt. Still he found it difficult to be 100 percent certain his intentions weren't self-motivated. Could be he needed to stop meddling in a situation he didn't understand.

&

Across town, Lauren lay in her own bed thinking about her life. Jake was right about one thing—she'd hidden from the world for years. They had sought answers only to find there weren't any. While medications helped regulate the frequency of her attacks, she had been forced to exist in the safe world created for her.

She couldn't pretend the problem didn't exist or that it would go away so she could live a normal life. Now was as normal as it was going to get for her and while she'd accepted that as a truth, she knew Jake thought there was potential for change.

But Lauren knew her limitations, and she wouldn't allow him to make her feel even more discontented with her boundaries. Feeling at peace with her decision, she fell asleep.

She called Jake the next morning. "Mom found a deal for you. Her friend has a daughter with a crib and changing table/dresser combination she wants to sell. It's a mahogany wood set she's selling for two hundred dollars. Her grandson is getting a big boy bed. He's the last child her daughter plans to have, so she wants to find a new home for the nursery furniture now. You interested?"

"Yes, ma'am."

"Hang on." She asked her dad a question. "Daddy says he'll go with you to pick it up. And Mom says we'll shop for Teddy's new room if you want."

"I'd appreciate that," he said without hesitation. "No cartoon characters, though. Trucks, cars, or animals are okay."

Lauren decided he must have had some sort of experience with the restricted items that he didn't care to repeat. Or else he intended to expose his son to a more masculine design.

They went to a big toy store and while they didn't find anything they liked, Lauren found a musical toy for Teddy's crib and a safety bath seat. They visited three more stores before finding the perfect nursery decorations. A few more must-have items made their way into the cart at each place.

Back at the house, Jake met them at the door, taking in the number of bags.

Jake studied the seat contraption that fell out of the bag Lauren carried. "I thought we agreed to nursery decorations."

"Teddy will love playing in the tub." She nodded to the item. "This will keep him safe."

"What else?" Jake asked.

"A little push car and a child swing to hang in a tree or off the porch."

Jake sighed and reached for his wallet. "I should have known better. I forget how much women love to shop."

Lauren grabbed his arm. "These are gifts for Teddy."

"I'm paying for the nursery items," he insisted.

Suzanne came up the steps carrying more bags. "You can pay for what you expected us to buy, but I warn you now these aren't going back." She held up a carrier bag. "I never got to buy clothes for little boys. Teddy will be so cute."

"Cute?" Jake teased with sudden good humor. "Shouldn't he be handsome?"

"Maybe when he's an old man like his daddy," Suzanne quipped. She pulled a pair of short denim overalls from the bag. "Look at these. They're a necessity now that he lives at the farm. I got a couple of different styles."

Jake laughed at her reason for the purchase.

"Teddy outgrows his clothes almost as fast as I buy them, so I'm sure he can use whatever you bought. Though I think we can guarantee he's all but on the best-dressed list if the number of bags counts for anything."

Greg came out onto the porch. "Where have you been? We've been back for hours."

Suzanne kissed him. "Our assignment was more complicated. We had to find our items, which involved visiting more than one store. Wait until you see these clothes, Greg. They are adorable."

"There's another of those words," Jake said.

Suzanne eyed him. "Well, he is cute and adorable, and I think if a woman told you the same thing, you'd preen a bit, Jacob Greer."

"You think?" he asked with a broad grin.

"I know. Is the crib set up?"

Greg nodded. "They had it in the garage but hadn't taken it apart." He grinned. "I thanked Scott for being too busy to handle the chore. We put it in your old room. It's good to go."

Suzanne shook her head. "Lauren, get those antibacterial wipes from the car. You two do what you were doing while we ready the nursery for our little guy."

Jake started to follow. "I'll help."

"Leave it to us. You'll like what we bought. If not, I will personally take everything back."

He waved his hand in invitation to continue.

"Oh, there's a bag of sub sandwiches in the car."

"I'll get them," Greg volunteered. "I'm starving."

Suzanne patted her husband's ample waistline. "I doubt that, but go ahead and eat. We'll have this finished in no time."

Two hours later, Lauren looked around the room and announced, "Instant nursery. That's really nice furniture."

"I'm so glad I remembered Doreen saying they planned to move Scottie to a big boy bed."

"Certainly Teddy's gain." Lauren eyed her mother. "You think Jake will like this?"

"What's not to like? It's got everything a boy's room should have and more. I love that glove beanbag chair."

Lauren nodded. "I can see Teddy crawling into it for naps. Hopefully Yapper won't decide it's a doggie bed."

"I don't think Jake will allow Yapper in here when Teddy's playing. He's too little to know how to play with her. I've noticed Yapper keeps her distance from Master Teddy's little hands." She stuck her head into the hall and called, "Gentlemen, come tell us what you think."

Jake carried the sleeping baby in his arms. His gaze moved around the room and he nodded approval. "I like the sports theme."

Lauren pulled back the comforter. "Here, lay him down."

Jake settled his son in the crib.

"We loved every minute of it. I hung his new clothes in the closet." Suzanne pulled open the door and lifted out a little dress outfit. "I got this for church."

He'd told them he planned to attend their church the next day. "Thanks to you two, Teddy will have to beat off the girl babies in the nursery."

Lauren couldn't help but think Teddy's dad might have to beat off some of the single church ladies. She found the thought rather disconcerting. The idea made her feel almost territorial. She'd spent entirely too much time with him in a different environment these past few days.

eight

Jake and Teddy showed up at Peace Church a few minutes early. He found Lauren sitting in her dad's car and asked, "Can you show us where the nursery is?"

"Sure."

"I left Yapper in the kitchen. I hope that's not a mistake. I walked her and made sure she had water."

"Chew toys?"

"Yes. Her own and one of Teddy's that she's mangled."

"I'm sure she'll be fine. Hey, Teddy," Lauren whispered as she touched the baby's stomach. "You look mighty handsome in that outfit." The oxford shorts and polo shirt were a perfect fit. He wore little rubber-soled sandals.

"I had a time getting him dressed. He wanted to play with all those new things in the nursery."

That pleased Lauren. "How did he sleep?"

"Woke once around four. I heard him on that baby monitor your mom bought. Then he went back to sleep and didn't wake again until seven or so."

"Is that a different schedule?"

"Oh yeah, the two of us spent restless nights in the same bed. Even though I pushed it up against the wall, I slept light to make sure he didn't roll off, and we woke each other during the night with our movement.

"We'll both rest better, though I think I might have one up on him with that new mattress. I can definitely give a testimonial to how comfortable it is. I'm going to have to take a set home with me. Give me a good reason to get home more often."

Lauren chuckled. "Let's take Teddy to the nursery, and you

can come to the singles class with me today."

❧

She knew from Jake's participation in the study that he had a good understanding of scripture. He obviously read and studied his Bible regularly, and it showed in his thought-provoking comments.

"Good to have you with us, Jake," their teacher, Conrad Little, said after class. "Come again."

The men shook hands, and the teacher moved on to speak with someone else. As Lauren expected, several women hurried over to welcome Jake. From her vantage point, she noted the way he smiled at them.

She wanted to push the other women out of his path and keep him completely for herself. She'd never experienced this before. *Don't be ridiculous*, she thought as he checked his watch and took her arm. They walked toward the sanctuary.

"Should I check on Teddy?"

"If he needs you, they'll post that number they gave you on the screen so you can come to the nursery. I'm sure he's enjoying himself."

They settled next to her parents. Suzanne leaned forward and patted Jake's hand. "Good to see you."

The music minister directed them to open their hymnals. Lauren sang but not loudly. She didn't fool herself that she had any musical talent. Her mother's voice had a beautiful lilting quality, but unfortunately she'd inherited her dad's vocal abilities.

After the song, the director indicated they should be seated. The pastor stepped up to the podium. "I see we have a number of visitors with us today. Welcome. Everyone, please extend the right hand of fellowship to those visitors."

The church erupted with people moving about to welcome visitors and speak to those whom they hadn't seen for a few days or a week. Several of her parents' friends came to be introduced to Jake. And other single women in the church took advantage of the opportunity to welcome him as well.

"You're a popular guy," Lauren said as they returned to their pew.

He opened and closed his hand. "Can't recall the last time I shook hands with so many people."

"Your church doesn't do that?"

He shook his head. "I visit churches wherever I am when my work schedule allows. I usually arrive in time for preaching."

She nodded, thinking how much she'd miss going to church each week.

"We have special music today," the music minister announced. The song was "One Touch." The Nicole C. Mullen song had always held special meaning for Lauren. She knew about being ostracized for something you couldn't control.

The service continued, the choir sang another song, they collected the offering, and the pastor stepped to the pulpit.

"I've had a number of requests for prayer this week," he began. "Members of our congregation are facing hardships and we've prayed for release from their pain and miracles for those who need them.

"If you'd like to open your Bibles and read along with me, starting with Matthew 14:36. 'And besought him that they might only touch the hem of his garment: and as many as touched were made perfectly whole.'

"We all pray for healing for loved ones." He paused and looked around the congregation. "And when those prayers seem to go unanswered, we feel let down, but I tell you our God is in the miracle business. We see them every day.

"This week I had a sister tell me she's been praying for a miracle for her friend. He's disabled and suffering great hardship, and she wanted nothing more than for him to be healed, to have his life back.

"As age goes, he's a relatively young man. Lots of life ahead of him. But she felt the prayer had gone unanswered until he told her the doctor said he's a walking miracle, that most people in his condition are wheelchair-bound. So you see she got her answer. Not the one she sought but still a miracle.

"An acceptable miracle? Better than nothing, you say. A gift from God, I tell you. He's given this young man mobility. Yes, he has this thorn to live with, the pain he suffers from, but he's also a believer. He attends church and reads his Bible and worships the God of love. And he knows that one day he will be freed of his pain because God promises him that.

"Our God is in the miracle business."

Cries of "amen" filled the room.

"Do we have the faith to believe in Jesus' ability to heal us? Listen to this, Matthew 17:20 says, 'Because of your unbelief: for verily I say unto you, If ye have faith as a grain of mustard seed, ye shall say unto this mountain, Remove hence to yonder place; and it shall remove; and nothing shall be impossible unto you.'

"Ask yourself this question. Do you have mountain-moving faith? Is your belief that you can be healed strong enough to remove that mountain of pain? That burden you bear? Will you glory in God's miracles in your life, or will you declare yourself destined to live with the affliction you bear?"

Did she? Had she stopped praying? Seeking God's healing? When had she lost hope?

Jake glanced at Lauren and she smiled wanly. Jake covered her hand with his. His touch made her feel so warm. Safe.

She turned her hand over and clasped his. Their hands remained entwined as the service continued.

God must have intended this sermon for her today. She couldn't claim faith that strong when she doubted her own ability to accomplish the dreams she'd revealed to Jake. Could she overcome her fears and live a full, contented life?

The service ended and Jake got to his feet. "Guess I'll head on home. Feed Teddy and check on Yapper."

"Can you find your way back to the nursery?"

He nodded. "Thanks for inviting me," he told Suzanne. "I enjoyed the service."

She hugged him. "I'm glad you came. We're going out for lunch. You want to come?"

"Not today. Thanks for asking."

He glanced at Lauren. "What are you doing later? I thought we might go exploring."

She had no plans. She could laze around the house, read, or watch television, but that didn't appeal. Nor would she ask her dad to take her over to the plant to catch up on the work she'd left undone while working on the house.

"We could take the ferry service over to Carrot Island," Lauren suggested. "Check out the beach, look for shells, and see the wild horses."

"Sounds like fun."

"They leave you on the island for a couple of hours so bring whatever Teddy needs for that time. I'll bring a beach sheet and water."

"What time?"

"Around one thirty? The ferry is just down the street. Be sure and put sunscreen on Teddy. We don't want him getting sunburned."

Both elected to wear shorts and sneakers. Lauren wore a knit top and Jake wore a T-shirt. He had dressed Teddy in a sunsuit and sneakers.

They arrived at the ferry service and when Lauren went to pay, Jake said, "My treat."

She shrugged and stuck the money back into her pocket. They walked along the wooden deck and down a steep plank to the dock where the ferry boat waited. Lauren climbed in, and Jake passed Teddy to her. She sat on the bench seat in the middle front. Jake joined her, placing the bag between his feet.

The captain told some people to shift to the other side of the boat and then backed around and headed slowly out to sea. "If you look over to your right, you'll see the dolphins."

They were rewarded with the view of a fin or sometimes a bit more of the dolphins at play.

They moved slowly through the wake and then picked up speed. Lauren held on to the silver bar along the side, feeling the splatter of water as they rode the waves.

The trip only took minutes. Lauren felt ungainly as she climbed off the front of the boat and stood on the beach. Jake passed over their things and then Teddy before following.

"The shells are over that rise and the horses are in the middle of the island, doing horse things," their captain said, adding a final warning. "Be back here in two hours when we return to pick you up."

Jake carried Teddy as they walked the area, keeping their distance as they watched the horses and then looked for shells.

Later they rested on the beach sheet at their drop-off point. Lauren placed a couple of nearly perfect shells she'd found on the sand next to her, planning to keep them as a reminder of their day together.

"Now I know what a castaway feels like," Jake said.

Lauren giggled. "Hey, maybe one day we can take the three-hour tour." They both remembered the old sitcom.

While they were not alone, the place had a feeling of isolation. The island rose out of the water, a mountain of sand with no beach, wild grasses, and trees.

"Do you do a lot of sightseeing when you travel?"

"I usually find a hotel close to where I work and then visit the nearby restaurants. I tried to go home every other weekend, so on the weekends I stayed, I would get out and visit the tourist sites that were recommended to me."

She used a shell to scoop and pile sand next to where she

sat, her legs stretched out before her. Teddy sat between them. "I've traveled a few times. Mom and I took a cruise once with church ladies and there were training sessions for the computers at the plant. I don't dare fly on my own. Heaven knows where I'd end up."

Jake smiled at that.

When Teddy tried to stand, Jake took the baby's hands in his, letting him sink his feet in the warm sand. He flopped on his bottom and grabbed handfuls of sand and cried when the wind tossed some into his face.

She dug through the bag for the wipes and handed the packet to Jake. "Did he get any in his eyes?" Lauren moved to help.

"I don't think so."

She handed him a bottle of water. "Here, wash his face just to be sure."

Afterward, Jake swung his son up on his shoulders. "Let's walk until the ferry arrives."

Teddy's hands tangled in Jake's hair. He winced. "Easy there, buddy. Don't yank your old man bald."

Lauren walked alongside, enjoying the feel of the warm sand beneath her bare feet. "You live in New Mexico?" At his curious look, she said, "I saw the address on the proposal. What about your family?"

"I have a brother who lives in Seattle. Dad died after a stroke, and Mom remarried a couple of years later. She and my stepfather split their time between Florida and Arizona. I don't see her as often as I'd like."

Lauren looked at him. "She doesn't want to see Teddy?"

"Every chance she gets. Mom visits when I'm home."

"What about your brother? Does he have a wife and children?"

"Ryan's had a couple of wives and has two boys with his second wife. Ryan Jr. and David are four and five. I haven't seen them in a while. We talk and threaten to visit each other, but it rarely happens."

"Threaten?"

"We aren't the closest brothers in the world. He's a few years older than I, and we defined sibling rivalry. Fought about everything."

Lauren felt a degree of sadness for this family that was so distant from each other. She loved her parents and couldn't imagine life without them. Even if she didn't live in their home, she wanted to be in the same area. If she'd been blessed with a sibling, she liked to think they would have been close as well.

Teddy yawned widely.

"Time for somebody's nap," she said.

"Yeah, he'll probably fall asleep right about time for the boat to pick us up."

They managed to keep Teddy awake until they arrived back at the car. Jake drove Lauren home.

"I'll be late in the morning. I want to see how Teddy and Yapper do. If everything works out, I'll be in. If not, I'll take the day off and drop them at day care on Tuesday."

"They'll like Mrs. Hart."

Jake looked hopeful. He'd met the woman briefly at church and she seemed nice. "Didn't you say you were friends with her daughter?"

Lauren nodded. Long ago, before the diagnosis, she'd been good friends with Melissa Hart, but that had ended when the girl decided she didn't want to be the freak's friend anymore. She couldn't blame her. School was hard enough without having your peers question your friends.

"I'll send up a prayer that all goes well. Thanks for this afternoon. It's been a nice change."

nine

She needed friends. Lauren came to that conclusion as she showered and changed into knit shorts and a top and went downstairs. The time with Jake and Teddy left her feeling energized and alive, ready for more fun.

Her mother looked up from her book. "Did you enjoy yourself?"

"I did. Jake plans to stay home in the morning to see how things go with Mrs. Hart. He's nervous. I hope it works out for them. He's very happy about the house."

Her mother nodded. "He wanted a home environment for his family. He'll have that at Mom's. I need to pick up the paint. He wants to get started. I told him there's no big rush. He's going to be there for a while."

"He's contracted for six months?"

"Mid-January, I think."

Much too soon, she thought, considering how much time had passed already.

After dinner, Lauren went to her room to read e-mail and play computer games on her laptop. She read her Bible for a while and then reached for her iPod.

She took it outside to the upper deck and sat in a rocker, enjoying the nice breeze. The moon glistened off the water and boats clanked in their moorings. She pushed the buds into her ears and started the mystery she'd downloaded from the library.

All too soon her eyes drifted closed. She gave up and went inside to prepare for bed.

❧

Ashleigh looked up and greeted her with a big smile.

"Good morning. Your mail's on your desk. There are a few things that need to be signed. I put in some requisitions for Jermaine on Friday for some items that need to be ordered. If you'll approve them, I'll call in the orders."

"I'll take a look." Lauren started for her office and almost as if she heard Jake whispering in her ear, turned back and asked, "How was your weekend?"

The young woman didn't miss a beat. "Pretty good. I had a blind date Friday night, but he's not going to work out. He was all about himself."

"I'm sorry."

Ashleigh grinned. "I'm not. Believe me, to know this guy was not to love him."

Lauren chuckled.

"What about you? Did you finish at the house?"

She nodded. "Mr. Greer and his son moved in Friday night."

"How old is his son?"

"Nearly nine months. A real cutie." She could see Ashleigh had more questions but wouldn't ask them. "Do you recall the name of that lady who wanted to do a feature on Sleep Dreams?"

Ashleigh thought for a moment and shook her head. "Want me to make some phone calls?"

"Check with Mrs. Ava and see if she remembers. Daddy got the inquiry, so she probably has the name in her message book."

"Are you thinking about doing the show?"

Lauren nodded. "Mr. Greer thinks the publicity would help sales."

"It can't hurt. Seeing how mattresses are made is pretty interesting."

Lauren started toward her office and stopped. "I need you to pull the time sheets for the past couple of years. Mr. Greer wants to review them."

Ashleigh grimaced. "Last year is in storage. I have the printouts here in the office. I can ask some of the guys to pull them."

"Hold up until I ask if he can use the printouts. Easier than combing through the time sheets."

Lauren spent her morning catching up. She checked and filed production reports, keyed payments, prepared the deposit, and gathered data Jake had requested.

Midmorning, Ashleigh came in with the name and number of the woman who had asked them to do the program. "Like you said, Mrs. Ava had the number logged into her message book."

"We should all be that organized." Her father had a true gem in the secretary who had worked for him since Lauren was a little girl.

She smiled up at her assistant. "Looks like I may get my fifteen minutes of fame doing promotion for Sleep Dreams."

"You don't sound very excited."

She eyed the paper and asked, "You ever dreamed of being a star?"

Ashleigh stifled a giggle. "Maybe when I was a teenager. No adult aspirations."

"I'm not excited," Lauren admitted. "Daddy's not about to do the program, and if I can't convince Mom, it's me. And I'm not television material."

"You'll do fine."

"If I don't have an attack."

"Don't think about it," Ashleigh advised.

"Hard not to but if I have to do this, I will."

Since his arrival, Jake had sent her thoughts off on all kinds of tangents. This television program for one. He'd been very encouraging. And basically all she had to do was talk about what she knew. Hadn't she run these floors since she was a child? All she had to do was answer questions and be personable while they filmed.

"I'm sure there won't be a problem," Ashleigh said.

"You may have to tag along with a really cold drink, but I'm going to call and see if they're still interested. If so, we're going to be on television."

❧

Within an hour of her arrival, Jake knew Mrs. Hart would be a good addition to their family. Teddy hadn't shown any of the stranger anxiety he'd been experiencing lately, and she thought Yapper was the cutest little thing she'd ever seen in her life.

Jake picked up his briefcase and keys. "I need to get to work. My cell and office numbers are on the fridge, and I've shown you where to find Teddy's things."

Mrs. Hart settled Teddy on her hip. "Does he have any food allergies?"

They had gone over his feeding and nap schedule. "None that I know about. He eats pretty much everything except mixed peas and carrots."

"Oh, but carrots are good for his eyes."

"He can eat carrot sticks when he's older. It's not worth the fight to get them in him now."

The woman looked to be about the same age as Suzanne Kingsley. Attractive, thin, and appreciative of the job. "Thank you for giving me this opportunity."

"Thank Suzanne Kingsley. She referred you."

"I have."

"Call if you need anything. We moved in Friday night so most of our stuff isn't unpacked."

"Would you like me to handle that for you? I'd be happy to work on it during Teddy's nap."

"How do you feel about laundry?" Jake asked, not yet comfortable with the scope of the job he had to create for the woman.

"I don't mind."

"Teddy's dirty clothes are in plastic bags in the utility

room. I planned to do them at the hotel but never got around to it."

"Do you have an iron?"

Jake shrugged. "I'm not sure what the Kingsleys left."

"Suzanne probably left an iron and board."

"I usually send my shirts out to the laundry."

"I did my husband's shirts. He always said I did a better job than the dry cleaner."

Jake wondered what had happened with the husband. The woman took a deep breath and answered his thought as though he had spoken it aloud.

"I suppose the new wife sends his stuff out. He traded me in for a younger model after the kids left for college."

"I'm sorry."

"Oh, don't be," Mrs. Hart said, waving her hand to negate the issue. "She didn't get any prize. He was a hard man to please. I suspect he was the reason my kids attended colleges across the country and took jobs so far away. Not having my kids close is much more difficult. Besides, I don't mind having no one to please but myself. Makes life easier. Oh, that's probably something I shouldn't say to my new employer. I'm sorry. TMI."

Jake grinned. "I appreciate anything you feel like doing. Of course, Teddy is your primary concern."

"Oh, no doubt about that, Mr. Greer."

"Call me Jake."

"You can call me Geraldine. Or Gerry. I answer to either one."

"Okay, Gerry, I'm off. Call if you need me. I'll be home around five thirty or so."

Jake went out to his car, glancing up to see them standing in the door. Gerry and Teddy waved good-bye. Jake waved back.

He paused in the driveway, pushing back his concern, but then he remembered the Kingsleys' recommendations for

Gerry Hart and felt reassured.

At the office, he stopped by to see Lauren. She waved him in, holding up a finger to indicate she would be another minute on the phone.

"Okay, Sarah, I look forward to seeing you on the twenty-fifth. I appreciate the opportunity to tell the Crystal Coast about Sleep Dreams."

Lauren wrapped up the conversation and hung up the phone. "I just made arrangements for them to come out and talk about what they want to cover on the show."

"That's good. It will make more people aware of what we have to offer."

"How did this morning go?"

"Gerry Hart and Teddy clicked right off. She even asked about doing other chores before I brought it up. I told her Teddy was her priority, but she could do anything she felt would help around the house. By the way, is there an iron? She asked and I didn't have a clue."

Lauren nodded. "In the laundry room. In the built-in ironing board cabinet."

"Okay. Good," he said, turning toward the door.

"Jake, hold on. About those time sheets. Ashleigh has the printouts where they were entered for computer payment, but the cards are in storage. Do you need the actual cards?"

"The sheets are fine. If she has any current time sheets, I'd like to take a look. We need to discuss the way the timekeeping is done."

"I'll have her bring them to your office."

"Anything else?"

"Ashleigh thinks I'll do okay on television. I'm still not sure."

"You'll never know if you don't try. Don't look for problems."

ten

Lauren's confidence level skyrocketed when she managed to get through the stressful event without an attack. Not that she'd been totally attack-free during the time leading up to the program, but she had survived what she thought would be the worst situation ever and felt proud of her accomplishment.

As first experiences went, it hadn't been as bad as she feared. Her mom had a scheduling conflict, and Lauren ended up on the other side of the microphone talking about Sleep Dreams. She'd taken Sarah Warren through the factory, showing how their mattresses were manufactured, even giving tips on how to care for mattresses.

Sarah had sent over a copy of the program, and Lauren watched it with her parents and Jake in the conference room.

"Good job, Laurie."

"Thanks, Dad."

"Very good," Jake agreed. "We need to look at doing some commercials to follow up on this."

"Well, now that we've got our own Miss Hollywood," her dad all but drawled, "I agree wholeheartedly."

"No way," Lauren cried. "You can peddle your wares just as well as I can."

The program aired a couple of days later.

"We saw you last night. You did a great job," Ashleigh enthused the next morning when she greeted Lauren with a big smile.

"Thanks." Curious, Lauren asked, "Who is *we*?"

"I had some friends over and when I told them they were doing a piece about Sleep Dreams, they watched with me.

You have an admirer."

Lauren did a double take.

"I told him you were out of his league, but he wouldn't let it go. I finally said I'd ask. I can tell him you're busy or something."

"What kind of guy is he?" She surprised herself with the question.

"He's okay."

"Just okay?" Not much of a recommendation for her new fan.

"I never considered him dating material," Ashleigh admitted. "He's not my type. We're having a pool party this weekend. If you thought you might want. . . You're welcome to come to the party."

You have to start somewhere, Lauren told herself. Why all of a sudden did she feel driven to make friends?

"I'd be there," Ashleigh continued. "I wouldn't let anyone. . . You know what I mean."

Lauren smiled at her assistant. "I appreciate that you look out for me. I probably don't tell you often enough, but having you outside my door helps me function in my crazy world."

"I don't really know what it's like to live with. . .the narcolepsy. It can't be easy."

"It's not unless you adapt to the situation." *Adapt.* She'd used Jake's word. "I pray a lot. And lately I've realized how deep I have my head buried in the sand. I don't have friends because I'm afraid of what they'll think when I have an attack. And we both know it's always when, never if."

"If they're good friends, they'll be concerned about you, not your problem," Ashleigh said without hesitation.

"Not everyone can handle it. Some people freak out. Some laugh. I need people who don't mind my problem. I know me being your boss makes our relationship different, but I thought maybe we could have lunch sometime. Or we could go out to dinner. Maybe even see a movie, though I don't know how long I'd last in a dark theater."

She grew quiet, and Lauren realized she'd put Ashleigh in a difficult situation. "It's okay. You don't want to deal with me in your off time."

Ashleigh frowned. "It has nothing to do with your condition. I like you, and what's more I respect you and all you've accomplished. I don't know that I would be as strong as you've been."

"I don't think of myself as strong." Lauren felt like a coward who hid out and limited her life.

If Jake hadn't asked those questions and shared some pretty brutal personal observations, she probably wouldn't be doing this now.

"Maybe we can eat lunch in the cafeteria. Jake says I need to socialize with the staff."

"Sure. Anytime."

"Thanks, Ashleigh." Lauren picked up her purse and lunch bag and walked toward her office.

"You should come to the pool party," Ashleigh called.

Lauren looked back and shook her head. "Too dangerous. People start playing around and next thing you know you're in the pool. I could drown."

"It can get rowdy. I hate it when they shove me in. Uh, Lauren," she began hesitantly, "Austin said he'd fix me up with this friend of his that I like if I introduced him to you. So if you want to meet him, we could double-date. See if these guys are worthy of us."

Ah, an ulterior motive. "Why do you think he wants to meet me?"

"He kept saying how pretty you were and asking why he'd never seen you before." She paused again. "I told him you were way too classy for him. I always tease the guys about being classless. They're not at all dignified like your dad and Mr. Greer. They're into partying and sports and acting stupid. I can't believe how juvenile they can be at times."

Her comment gave Lauren pause. She wasn't into any of that either. "Daddy likes sports. Of course he's much older than your friends and has Mom to keep him in line."

Ashleigh laughed. "Yeah. Behind every good man there's a good woman."

Lauren nodded. "What's that old saying? Something about kissing a lot of frogs before finding your prince?" Not that she planned to do any kissing anytime soon. She'd need to know the guy really well before that happened.

"Yeah, and some of them are big, old, ugly toad frogs with attitude."

"Where do you meet guys?"

"Mostly at clubs and on the beach. I met Austin Danforth at college. We take the same night class."

Well, that said something for him, Lauren thought.

"He plans to get his degree and move out of sales. He said with the economy being like it is now, car sales are tough."

Times were difficult, but they had to hold firm and believe things would get better.

Then her thoughts shifted to Jake and the way he encouraged her to make friends. Did that include dating? What would it hurt to meet this guy?

"If you don't mind double-dating, I'd like to meet your friend."

"Okay," Ashleigh declared enthusiastically. "Is there a night that's better for you?"

"Friday or Saturday?"

"Should I tell him about your condition?"

Lauren shook her head. She didn't want total strangers aware of her situation. Later, if things worked out, she'd fill him in herself.

"Probably best until you get to know him. Things might not work out, and that's not the kind of information you want him sharing. Would you like for him to call or e-mail you?"

"Let's do the double date. I'll meet him then."

"I'll get back to you with a date and time."

"Meanwhile you can tell me everything you do know about him. Do you have pictures?" Lauren covered her mouth. "That sounds superficial."

Ashleigh shook her head. "Not at all. Seeing him might answer some of your questions. I'll bring one."

Safe in the privacy of her office, Lauren considered the step she'd taken. Driving lessons, the discussion over the house, and now a date with a stranger. Yep, her parents would think she'd lost her mind. And she wasn't so sure they wouldn't be right.

She wanted to say Jake Greer was her motivation for making changes in her life but thought perhaps voicing her desires had been the motivator.

Ashleigh came in around noon the next day with an invitation.

"Let's go to lunch and I'll tell you what I know about Austin."

"I brought lunch today, but there's enough for both of us." Lauren didn't share that she'd thought maybe Jake would stop by so she'd added an extra cup of soup to the thermos and packed a sandwich for him.

"Want me to run to the cafeteria for iced teas?"

"Sounds good. Unsweetened decaf for me."

After she left, Lauren moved a pile of folders from her small conference table and found two mugs for the soup. She spread the food on the table and pulled a roll of paper towels from the cabinet.

"Looks good," Ashleigh commented as she settled opposite Lauren.

"The soup is Mom's specialty. She watches the Food Network when she can and is always trying some new recipe." Lauren bowed her head to say grace and picked up her spoon.

Ashleigh took a taste and nodded. "Do you cook?"

Lauren smiled at that. "With supervision. I don't dare try it on my own. I could burn the house down. I do like to bake. Which I'm sure accounts for the fifteen pounds I can't lose."

"I don't cook much," Ashleigh said. "It's easier to eat out."

She unwrapped the cold-cuts sandwich and offered Ashleigh half. "We probably wouldn't cook as much if it weren't for Daddy. He's not likely to let a night go by without meat and potatoes on the table."

"I suppose a husband motivates a woman to prepare meals."

Lauren laughed outright at that. "Love motivates women to do a lot of stuff. Brings out the homemaker in us."

"None of the men I meet make me feel the least domestic."

They ate for a few minutes before Lauren asked, "What brought you here?"

"Former boyfriend was in the military. I followed him to North Carolina and liked the area enough to stay when the relationship fizzled. Sometimes I miss my parents and Savannah, but I like the area and my work. What about you? Do you like your work?"

Lauren considered the question. "I do. Though I doubt I could find another company that would tolerate my condition."

"You work so hard. I did some reading about narcolepsy after coming to work for you, but it's hard to understand."

Hard to live with, too, Lauren thought. "None of us understood what was happening until the doctors diagnosed the problem."

"And they don't know why you developed it?"

"There's no definitive answer. I live with it. I suppose you could call what I do living. Some might say I exist."

"Don't say that, Lauren. You have impressive accomplishments given what you face on a daily basis."

"Thanks." They had worked together for a couple of years now, but she'd never seen this aspect of her assistant. Lauren scooped some of the veggies from the mug.

Ashleigh pushed the photos across the table to her.

Lauren wiped her hands before accepting the pictures.

"He's six feet tall with brown hair and brown eyes. He has a pretty good build. Jogs five miles every morning. Claims he feels lousy if he doesn't."

"Uh-oh."

They grinned at each other.

Lauren wasn't a morning person nor did she jog. She didn't do much exercise for that matter. Like most people, her greatest motivation came around the New Year when she resolved to do better but quickly slid back into her old ways after a few days. She did walk Fred occasionally, but that hardly qualified as exercise.

"He tries to get us to run with him, but no one is interested."

"What else?" Lauren prompted.

"He's a transplant like me."

"From where?"

Her forehead creased. "California, I think."

That caught Lauren's attention. "He's a long way from home."

"He came here for a girl he met online. Found out all was not as it seemed."

Both Ashleigh and Austin had changed their lives for another person, and it hadn't worked out for them. Would she give up the life she knew and leave her family behind for the possibility of love? In her case, leaving her world behind could cause serious problems if she couldn't depend on the man she chose.

"Why didn't he go back home?"

Ashleigh shrugged. "Same as me, I think. We like the beach. He's a nice guy, Lauren. A good friend."

She wouldn't mind a good friend. "I look forward to meeting him."

Lauren rose and took their cups into the bathroom to rinse

and dry them with a paper towel. Ashleigh swept the crumbs into the palm of her hand and disposed of them along with the sandwich wrappers.

"This has been fun," she said. "Let's do it again. Next time I'll bring lunch."

Lauren grinned and said, "Anytime you want."

eleven

"Teddy and I were talking, and he thinks it's time for another driving lesson now that I've got your grandfather's Jeep running again."

Lauren's eyes widened at his words. When Jake stepped in her office that morning, she'd expected nothing more than business as usual.

Over two weeks had passed since Jake and Teddy moved into Gram's house. The past week had been hectic with regular work and meetings with Jake and her dad to discuss company improvements. And then today, out of the blue, he'd come up with this. "And how did Teddy say that?"

His grin did all kinds of things to Lauren's heartbeat.

"Well, actually I suggested it and he clapped his hands. He thinks we should make plans for this weekend." Jake spoke in a casual jesting way.

"You got Gramps's Jeep running?" When had he found the time? Her mom said he'd painted the rockers and swing, too.

"Yeah. Suzanne said it was okay. We'll throw Teddy's car seat into the back and go cruising."

Horror filled Lauren at the thought. "No. That's too dangerous."

Jake ignored her comment. "We can picnic under that big old tree."

"Are you listening to me?" She didn't like being steamrollered, and that was exactly what Jake was doing. And even worse, he expected her to fall in with his plans without argument.

The blue-green gaze pinned her. "If I doubted your ability, I wouldn't suggest this."

She stood up, surprised and more uncertain than ever. "My driving is too erratic. It can't be good for him."

"Don't you intend to drive anyone else around?"

The printer stopped and she reached for the pages. She glanced over the numbers, avoiding his question.

"Lauren?"

"I don't know." The truth gushed from her. "I have mixed feelings. Hurting myself would be bad enough, but harming others would be devastating."

He looped his arm about her shoulder, giving her a gentle squeeze. "If you don't believe in yourself, no one else will."

Jake's comment cut deep. "It's only with God's grace that I've accomplished anything in life."

The realization struck hard. Had she asked God to help her with these plans she was suddenly fast-tracking? And why wasn't she doing that? She'd always prayed first.

She needed to be certain she was doing what Jesus wanted for her. He'd helped her accomplish all she had in life and if this was His intention, He'd help her through.

Jake's encouragement and her parents' responses to her shared dreams had been wonderful. And she'd be the first to admit the idea of driving herself anywhere was fantastic. But where would she be when she got there? She didn't like being alone when an attack occurred. "I'm not comfortable with Teddy in the car."

"What about me?"

"I shouldn't risk your life, either." Lauren watched him as she said, "Perhaps I should drive myself around the farm until I feel more comfortable."

"No way."

The words exploded from him and Lauren wondered why. "Are you afraid I'll fall asleep and hurt myself?"

"No, I'm not."

"You should be."

Jake sighed. "It's important that you have someone there

to help when things happen and you don't know what to do."

"Like getting stuck in the sand on that first driving lesson?"

"Exactly. I pushed and you drove. You can't do both."

He had a point. "Okay, but I'll find a babysitter."

"Don't ask your mom. She already has so much to do."

She hadn't thought about whom she'd ask. Maybe no one and then she could put off the driving experience. "I could ask Ashleigh. We ate lunch in the cafeteria today."

He nodded approval, and she debated telling him about the plans. What would he think? Oh why not. Hadn't he encouraged her to get out there and meet people? "The television program had more results than expected. One of my fans wants to meet me."

A strange expression fleeted across his face. "What do you mean by 'fan'? You're not seriously considering meeting with a complete stranger, are you?"

Lauren shrugged. "Yeah, you meet strangers and sometimes they become friends. Actually this guy is a friend of Ashleigh's. We're going on a double date. She promised to stay nearby."

"Be careful. Some people aren't what they seem."

"I won't take any chances."

"Let me know about the driving lesson. Maybe Sunday after church. I thought we'd pick up a bucket of chicken and sides. Teddy can eat mashed potatoes."

After he left, her thoughts went to how carefree Jake sounded. Just the idea of having Teddy in the back of a vehicle while she drove scared her senseless. At least Jake could react in the event of an accident. Teddy wouldn't stand a chance.

≈

Lauren had a date. The words repeated themselves in his brain as Jake moved down the hall to his office. As he flopped down in his chair, it hit him that he didn't like the idea at all.

Sure, he'd encouraged her to make friends, but this wasn't what he meant. He particularly didn't care for the idea of her risking getting her heart broken by some guy who might not understand her problem. But what right did he have to interfere?

In a short time, he and Teddy would move on to the next job. He liked Lauren and if things were different, he could be interested in pursuing a relationship with her, but she needed more than he could give.

Still, he didn't have to like the idea. Maybe they could discuss it this weekend, and he could determine how comfortable she was. Was she taking the step because he'd pushed her to expand her horizons? Had he done the right thing?

He couldn't be sure. The worst thing would be for her to become discontented and depressed with the life she had because of something he'd said. Yes, he definitely would talk with her.

Jake smiled when he found Lauren waiting by his vehicle after church services on Sunday.

"I still don't know why I let you talk me into this."

His brows lifted. "Because you can't refuse really good fried chicken."

She laughed as she pulled her seat belt into place. "Yeah, the chicken motivated me."

"And the driving experience will, too."

"I didn't find anyone to watch Teddy."

"I've got it under control."

He'd asked Gerry to come over that afternoon. She'd be there by two thirty. That would give them time to change and have lunch.

Jake understood Lauren's concern and appreciated that she cared enough not to endanger his son. He stopped at the restaurant and ran inside to pick up the order. After stowing it behind his seat, he drove toward home.

He parked and Lauren carried their lunch bag inside. Jake carried Teddy with the diaper bag slung over his shoulder. She placed the bags on the counter and moved to take Teddy from his arms.

"He needs to be changed," Jake said. "We'll be right back."

He moved the guard blocking the doorway and carried Teddy down the hall to his room. After changing his son into the overalls, Jake left him in the crib while he exchanged his suit for jeans shorts and a golf shirt.

Back in the kitchen, he found Lauren had changed into capris and a print top.

"You are so cute in those," Lauren cooed to Teddy.

Teddy grinned and reached for her. Lauren took him. Jake noted that as she'd become more familiar with the baby, she'd grown more comfortable in handling him.

"Hey, buddy." She hugged him close. "Did you have fun in the nursery today?"

Teddy chattered nonsense for a few minutes before he chanted, "*Dadadada*." Lauren glanced over her shoulder to where Jake worked at the counter. "Your son's calling you."

"I hear." He screwed the top on a sippy cup and handed it to Teddy.

"I thought you planned a picnic?"

"Change in plans." He took Teddy's bowl from the drain tray and scooped mashed potatoes, added a little gravy, and asked, "You want to feed him?"

"Sure."

Jake pulled the high chair over to the table, and Lauren settled Teddy and tied on his bib. When she bowed her head to say grace, Jake did the same and listened to Teddy babble along with her.

She scooped potatoes into his mouth and smiled when Teddy decided he liked the food and reached for the spoon. "You want to feed yourself?"

"Not potatoes and gravy," Jake warned. "Last time he

rammed his hands in the bowl and had them all over everywhere."

She chuckled. "Did he get any into his mouth?"

"That might have been the only place he missed."

Lauren fed the baby more potatoes. "He's growing so fast. When's his birthday?"

"November twenty-fourth."

She nodded. "So tell me about this change in plans."

Jake eyed her before he spoke. "I asked Gerry to come over. But not because I don't trust you," he added.

Lauren touched Teddy's cheek. "He's so precious. I'd die if I hurt one hair on this head."

"What about my head?"

"Yes, you, too. There's no guarantee something won't happen."

He shrugged. "There's no guarantee for anyone who drives. I suspect you'll be more attentive than most."

"I'd like to think so, but then I know I can get sidetracked as easily as the next person."

"We're safe here, and you'll become more confident as you develop your skills."

"I hate to waste your time. Take time away from this little guy." She used Teddy's bib to wipe a bit of mashed potatoes from his chin.

He glanced at his son. "We'll go during his nap and have some fun after he wakes up. I think he wants you to push him around in that little car you bought him. It's killing my back."

"I should have gotten a wagon." Lauren placed the bowl on the table, out of the baby's reach. "That's all the potatoes he's going to eat."

Jake took a banana from the fruit bowl, deftly sliced it in half, and then cut that into bits, which he spread on the high-chair tray. Teddy demonstrated his pincer grasp and pushed the banana into his mouth.

"Fruits and veggies. You start them out eating right and all too soon they're existing on junk food."

Jake tapped her arm. "Stop being philosophical and come fix yourself a plate."

Lauren peered down into the box and chose a chicken breast. After scooping potatoes and cole slaw onto her plate, she opted to skip the biscuit.

They sat at the kitchen table. Teddy ate a few more banana bits before he grew tired and started to cry.

Jake wiped Teddy's face and hands and settled him on the living room carpet with a couple of toys. He waited to see if his son was content before returning to the table.

"This grilled chicken is actually pretty good." He held the drumstick in the air. "I eat way too much fast food, but every now and then I get the urge to eat right. Actually I have the urge pretty often but can't summon the enthusiasm to cook.

"At least Teddy has a decent diet now. You're right, though. I need to clean up my act before he starts eating regular food. Nutritionally balanced meals won't hurt either of us. So are you excited about your date?"

He could see his sudden change of subject startled her.

"I don't know much about the guy."

"You didn't know me either," Jake pointed out. "And here we are, two friends sharing Sunday lunch. Think of the date the same way."

Lauren dropped her fork on the plate. "It's not the same." She dropped her gaze. "You don't have expectations at the end of our lunches or dinners."

He felt his jaw tense. "He shouldn't either."

"Ashleigh says he's nice."

"I hope you have a good time." Did he really? He hoped she wasn't going too fast.

"No expectations, no disappointment if it's not what I hoped for." She glanced around and asked, "Where's Yapper?"

"Good question." He'd left her in the kitchen. Jake noticed

the lower corner of the guard he'd used to block the laundry room was pushed back. He spotted the tiny dog curled up on the pile of laundry he'd planned to wash the previous evening.

"Yapper," he called, moving the guard. She jumped up, coming over to dance about his feet as they walked back into the kitchen. "I'm surprised she didn't hear us. Must have worn herself out playing while we were gone."

The tiny dog barked nonstop as she made a wild dash into the living room. Yapper dodged Teddy's hands as she lapped at his face and then ran into the kitchen to jump up on Lauren's leg.

She wiped her hands and patted the dog's head. Her greeting served to excite the dog even further and she began to bark.

"Yapper, stop that," Jake demanded. "That yippy little bark drives me crazy."

"Poor baby can't help how she sounds," Lauren crooned as she patted her once more. "It's how she communicates."

"Quiet, Yapper," Jake snapped.

The dog looked at him with her big sad eyes.

"Why does her barking bother you so much?"

He was transported back in time to the day Gwen died. As usual, they argued over his refusal to give up his consulting job, and he had retreated to his home office and closed the door. Gwen had gone to swim in their heated pool while Teddy napped. Yapper's constant barking served as the impetus that forced him outside. He found the dog paddling furiously to keep her head above water while Gwen floated facedown in the pool.

He'd tried to resuscitate her, but it had been too late. The determination had been accidental death by drowning. The police thought she'd probably tripped over the dog, knocked herself unconscious when her head hit the pool coping, and drowned when she fell into the pool.

Jake felt a tremendous load of guilt. Not only had he been angry with his wife, he'd possibly provided the weapon that killed her.

"Jake?"

"She never stops."

"Teddy cries continually at times. Does that bother you?"

"No," he admitted gruffly.

The dog ran off. Lauren glanced into the living room and saw Teddy and Yapper engaged in a war over a stuffed toy. She laughed as the two waged battle. Like every tug-of-war, one would get ahead and then the other, until Teddy shook his head and yelled, "No."

That surprised the animal, and Teddy yanked his toy back to safety. Yapper danced around out of reach.

"Those two are quite a pair."

Jake nodded grimly. "You'd think Yapper would be afraid Teddy would grab her. He's got his hands on her a time or two, and she howled like he was killing her."

Yapper grabbed the other toy and ran off. Teddy crawled after her in hot pursuit.

"Look at him go."

The dog abandoned the toy in favor of dancing from side to side and barking at the baby. Teddy waved his arm and told her no again.

"He learned that from you." She started to laugh when Teddy chanted, "*Nonono.*"

Jake joined in and their laughter turned into deep belly laughs. The glass she'd been drinking from hit the floor.

He grabled her arm to keep her from falling off the chair. The attack passed in a couple of minutes. Lauren could hear Jake, felt his support as he kept her from falling out of the chair. It only lasted a couple of minutes.

"What happened?" he demanded, his arms wrapped about her.

"They call it cataplexy."

"Has it happened before? What caused it?"

"Yes. Probably caused by the laughter."

"Laughter?"

"I haven't laughed like that in a long time."

He could see she was angry at herself for being embarrassed. "Lauren, I'm sorry."

"It's not your fault. Laughing is an ordinary everyday activity."

"Do you need a doctor?"

"No, but I won't try to drive today."

"We can do something else. I'll call Gerry and let her know we don't need her. We can go for a drive. I know. Let's go see the Cape Lookout Lighthouse."

"We need to plan that for when we have a full day. We would have to catch a ferry over."

"I could take you home to rest."

"Yeah, I really need more rest."

Her sarcastic response bothered him. "I'm sorry, Lauren."

"Stop saying that. You didn't do anything," she snapped. "Sorry. I don't mean to be hateful. The experience still scares me."

"You've had these attacks before?"

"Not often. They're generally brought on by emotion."

"Should you call your mom?"

"There's nothing she can do."

He watched her closely. "Then what do we do, Lauren?"

"Next time I don't laugh so hard when I find something funny. See, there are reasons I subdue myself. Obviously I can't handle anything more."

Sadness touched his face. "Tell me you're okay. That this hasn't caused any harmful side effects."

"It's over, Jake. Let me clean up this mess before Teddy or Yapper gets into it."

"I'll handle it."

Withdrawn, she muttered, "Maybe you should take me home."

He grabbed a handful of paper towels and wiped up the tea. Jake stepped on the can lift and tossed the towels into the trash. "No. Your parents aren't there." He knew they had gone out for lunch with friends and planned to play pinochle that afternoon. "Teddy and I like having you around, so if we don't do anything but sit in the porch swing, we want you to stay."

"You have better things to do."

"I spend my Sunday afternoons doing what I like and today that's spending time with you."

She jumped up from the chair. "Don't do me any favors, Jake."

He caught her shoulders. "Stop it, Lauren. Did you take your medication today?"

"I don't know. I'd have to check my pillbox. Maybe it was relief in not having to drive with Teddy in addition to the laughter."

"So you think I caused your reaction?"

She wouldn't look him in the eye.

He didn't hear Teddy's babbling and glanced over to where his son pulled magazines from the rack. Yapper chewed furiously on Teddy's toy.

Lauren's gaze followed Jake's. She rose from the chair and went into the living room. "Bad dog," she chastised, taking the toy from him. "This is not yours." She picked Teddy up and moved to the sofa. "You should call Mrs. Hart."

"Sure you don't want to try driving?"

"I don't know what happened, and I'm not about to get behind the wheel of a vehicle and see if it happens again. That would be like playing Russian roulette with a fully loaded gun." Lauren's quiet but firm response left Jake with no doubt to her feelings on the matter.

Jake lifted Teddy from her arms. "I'll put him down for his nap and give Gerry a call. We'll hang out here. Maybe even go for ice cream later if you're up to it."

"Oh, I'm always up for ice cream."

After Jake left the room, Lauren went into the kitchen. She put away the leftovers and wiped down the table and high chair, pushing the chair back into the corner of the room. Teddy's bib lay on the floor. She picked it up and flaked off a bit of dried potato.

There were spots on the wall and cabinet where the tea had splashed. Finding a sponge underneath the sink, she wiped them off and debated cleaning the floor, which felt sticky. She located a mop in the laundry room and used it to clean the floor.

Had her fear brought on the attack? The laughter? She had been terribly afraid that Jake would insist on carrying through with his plan. What was he thinking? They'd had one lesson. Things had gone well, but that didn't mean every time would be the same.

Unbidden tears tracked along her cheeks. There were no guarantees in her life. No certainties.

Lauren understood the same could be said for everyone, but the balances didn't always make sense to her. Here tiny Teddy had lost his mother and Jake his wife, and yet she with all her flaws lived on. A misfit in a world that would never understand her.

At her feet, Yapper whimpered as if she understood Lauren's pain.

Tired of the maudlin thoughts, she swiped her eyes with the back of her hand. While her purpose might not be clear to her, it was clear to God. He had a reason, and it wasn't hers to question.

She picked up the little dog and pulled her to her chest, feeling comforted by her closeness.

❧

After Teddy sprawled comfortably in the crib, Jake stepped out into the hall. He pulled the cell from his pocket and dialed.

"Gerry, Jake here. Hope I caught you before you left."

"I'm still at home."

"Good. There's been a change in plans. You don't need to come after all. I'll pay you for this afternoon."

"You will not."

He leaned against the wall. "It's the least I can do for changing your plans."

"I didn't have plans. I went to church, picked up lunch, and came home."

"Well, now you can relax and prepare for next week with the terrible twosome."

She laughed. "They're not terrible."

"They keep us on our toes."

"That they do. See you in the morning."

Jake found Lauren on the sofa, thumbing through the Sunday paper he'd left on the coffee table.

"She hadn't left yet."

Lauren laid the paper down.

He sat next to her and sprawled comfortably on the sofa. She had picked up the magazines, put the toys in a basket, and straightened the kitchen. They sat in silence for a minute or so before Jake asked, "Lauren, do you feel I'm pushing you to step outside your comfort zone?"

There, he'd said it. Put his concern out there for consideration. He could see from her expression that she was uncomfortable with the question. "You do," he announced glumly.

"No, Jake. You encouraged me when I opened up to you about my dreams. And you've done what you could to make them happen. I don't understand why it's so important to you, but I appreciate the encouragement you've offered."

Why was it important? What purpose had he served by offering to teach her to drive? Revealing her secret desires to her parents? Pushing her to do the television program? Suggesting she find friends?

She wasn't Gwen. Lauren's decisions weren't based on being a healthy young woman who could do anything her heart desired. Not only was she forced to consider the ramifications of how narcolepsy affected her life in every decision she made, but she had to consider what could happen to her if she chose wrongly.

He had even suggested she rip herself from the safety of her parents' home. The one place in the world where she could feel secure. Why had he blinded himself to that? Needy women. He'd dealt with that with Gwen. He liked Lauren and didn't want to see her fall into the same trap. He'd encouraged her to pursue her dreams. Was that so wrong?

"Jake?"

"Sorry," he muttered, shaking himself from his reverie. "I was thinking about what you said earlier. You told me you weren't comfortable, but I insisted. I should have realized the stress wouldn't be good for you. I'm sorry, Lauren. That was wrong of me."

After a few minutes, Lauren spoke, "Sometimes the faith others have helps us to try a little harder. I think maybe I, along with Mom and Dad, reached a consensus that my life is the best it can be. I contented myself with the status quo even though I have dreams and aspirations. Maybe not as big as some people's, but I do have hope for the future. I don't see myself leaving Sleep Dreams, but you're right. Mom and Dad aren't always going to be there. I need to be practical and think about the future."

"No, Lauren. You don't. Both of your parents are healthy, active people who will be around for years. You don't need me pushing you to change your life."

"Is this because of what I said earlier? About the driving?"

He shrugged. "That and the feeling that I came on too strong. I don't live your life, Lauren. I have no right to say what you can and can't do."

She stared at him and then recited, " 'Doing what you've

always done gets you what you've always gotten.' Isn't that what you told us?"

He had said that and he'd meant it from a business perspective. Companies had to change constantly or become stagnant. He supposed people did, as well.

"I think you're a great encourager, but then improving quality of life is what you do."

Was it? Jake wondered. He certainly hadn't improved his family's life. Doing what he'd always done hadn't helped his marriage, and he knew it wouldn't help his son either. As Teddy grew older, he would need roots. A steady home environment where he could develop properly.

Not now, Jake thought. Teddy was a baby. It would be years before he would be forced to make a decision that would keep him in one place.

"I placed added stress on you," Jake said. "You need to tell me when it's too much. You did such a great job with the television program that the newspaper wants to do a feature. Your dad suggested you do the interview."

He felt her shiver with a frisson of fear.

"I'll do it. We have to keep the Sleep Dreams name out there to increase our profit margin."

"Tell me about the Christmas in July sales event," Jake suggested, hoping to distract her from their earlier conversation. "Greg said it was your idea."

Lauren rested one foot up on the old coffee table. "People fix up their homes for the holidays. The ad promotion had to do with getting new bedding before the guests arrive. We offered six months same as cash and promised their custom-made mattresses would be in place before the holidays. Sales were good. Some people elected to take warehouse inventory while others wanted custom. We're about two-thirds complete on the custom purchases."

"Well in advance of the deadline. Any other ideas?"

"I thought we might have a Snuggle sale in October."

"Snuggle?"

She laughed. "Winter is coming and people like to be warm and cozy in their beds. We could offer flannel sheets or a duvet with every purchase."

"What about Valentine's Day? Give your sweetheart a mattress."

Lauren's mouth widened with her smile. "Now that would be very different from flowers and candy."

Teddy cried out. "Nap's over," Jake said. "Ready for ice cream?"

"Let's go for a walk," she suggested. "I'm sure Yapper could use one and I know I could."

"Okay, we'll be right back. Yapper's leash is in the laundry room."

twelve

Lauren sat at her desk considering the previous afternoon. The walk had been fun. Jake explained that Yapper had a tendency to chase after wild animals, and he kept her on a leash to keep her out of trouble.

"She's got the heart of a lion," Lauren defended.

The little dog pranced and prowled as they walked along the dirt road that bordered the perimeter of the farm. Later, they went for ice cream and ate their favorite flavors from bowls. Teddy smacked his enjoyment of the icy treat.

She considered Jake's concern that he'd pushed too hard. She needed that push. Shove, actually. She wouldn't have reached out to Ashleigh nor done any of the other things she'd tried since meeting him.

Her assistant tapped on the door and came into the office. "You have plans for Friday night? The guys want to take us to dinner."

"I'm free."

"What if I come over and they pick us up at your place? Or we could meet them at the restaurant."

"Have them come to the house. Will he be weird about meeting my parents? I know they'll want to meet him and know where we're going. I don't think they'll show up at the restaurant, but you never know."

Ashleigh giggled. "I promise to look out for you. I'll stick by you like glue."

"And they'll bring us home pretty quickly."

She shrugged. "If they don't understand, too bad."

Lauren smiled at her. "Just remember, they don't know the whole story."

The week flew past and all too soon, Lauren was fighting back the butterflies in her stomach as she waited for her date to arrive. Her mother had taken her shopping the previous evening.

"Mom, I have plenty of clothes."

Suzanne shook her head. "You need something new. It's not every day a girl goes on her first date."

She groaned. First date. She sounded like a teen, not a twenty-seven-year-old woman.

"Where are they taking you?"

"Ashleigh suggested Clawson's 1905."

It was just down the street from her parents' home, and they loved to eat at the beautifully restored restaurant.

Lauren tried on a pile of clothes and came away with a cute top to wear with her black dress slacks and a pair of wedge heels. She refused to wear stilettos.

"Men like heels on a woman. Particularly when they wear a skirt."

Her mother was determined to get her into a dress. "Well, I don't plan to show him my legs or my teeth."

Suzanne roared. "Okay, I know when to shut up."

Now Lauren tugged at her clothing, which suddenly seemed not to fit properly.

"Stop that," her mother chided, slapping at her hands. "You look fine."

She glanced over into the family room where Jake and Teddy sat talking to her father. "What are they doing here?"

"Jake brought over some papers for your dad. I invited him to stay for supper."

Lauren rolled her eyes. Wasn't it bad enough that her parents had to sanction her blind date? Now Jake would be here watching. She bit the inside of her lip and steeled herself to deal with the situation.

The doorbell rang and Ashleigh breezed in, dressed in a short black dress guaranteed to impress her date. Lauren felt frumpy in comparison.

"You look great," Ashleigh declared.

"Thanks," Lauren mumbled.

"She does, doesn't she, Mrs. Kingsley?"

"Yes, Ashleigh, she does. Of course she didn't believe me when I told her."

"You look very pretty, Laurie." Jake stood in the doorway.

She blushed and offered him a self-conscious smile.

Teddy bounced in his father's arms, a smile on his face as he reached for her. *"Lalalala!"*

"He wants to say hello," Jake said as they came closer.

"Hey, sweetie," she said, taking him into her arms. She sat in the armchair and bounced him on her legs. "Did you have a good day with Mrs. Hale?"

Teddy jabbered. He reached for the decorations on her shirt and tried to pluck the tiny beads with his fingers. She patted them and asked, "Do you like my beads?"

He patted them with his hands.

Lauren pointed to the embroidery on his overalls. "Puppy."

Teddy touched it and chattered something that didn't sound like *puppy*.

In all the commotion, she didn't hear the doorbell and looked up to find Ashleigh standing there with two men.

She smiled shyly and got to her feet. Jake reached for his son. "Go get him," he whispered softly.

She grinned at him.

"Austin Danforth, this is Lauren Kingsley."

"Hello, Lauren," he said with a huge smile as he engulfed her smaller hand in his. "It's a pleasure to meet you."

"You, too." She quickly introduced her parents, Jake, and Teddy. He shook hands with her mother and father and nodded at Jake before smiling at the baby.

"Hi there, little guy. I have a nephew about your age."

Teddy continued to chant his version of Lauren's name and struggled to reach her.

"No, Teddy," Jake said, pulling the baby up in his arms. "Laurie has to go."

He wailed inconsolably. Suzanne took him. "Come on, sweetie. Let's check on dinner."

She paused to kiss her daughter's cheek and said, "Have fun, Laurie. Nice meeting you, Austin."

"You, too, Mrs. Kingsley. Ready?" he asked Lauren.

She nodded and paused by the entrance hall table to unplug her phone and tuck it into her purse.

Austin walked next to her on the sidewalk. "I've been looking forward to this all week."

He paused to open the passenger door and pulled the seat forward so the other couple could climb into the back.

"Me, too," Lauren said. His easy chatter made her comfortable.

Austin helped her inside and closed the door. He climbed into the driver's seat.

"Ashleigh tells me you're the CFO for your father's company," he commented as he drove the short distance to the restaurant.

"Among other things. It's a small company. We all wear a number of hats."

"You did a great job on the television program. I'm thinking of ordering a custom mattress."

"I'd never done anything like that before. The interviewer was really good. I followed her lead, and the time flew by. I didn't want to do the program, but Jake said it would be good publicity."

"Jake? The guy at the house?"

"Yes. He's working with us to improve operations."

Austin glanced at her and moved his gaze back to the road. "The little boy belongs to him?"

"Yes," Lauren said.

"He really likes you."

"I'm fond of him, too," she admitted.

His look became a little speculative. "You spend a lot of time with him?"

"Not a lot." She didn't want to talk about how often she saw Teddy or Jake. Lauren changed the subject. "Ashleigh tells me you're a car salesman."

"Yes." He named the dealership where he worked. "I've been there for about two years now. I'm working on getting my BA so I can pursue a different field. Maybe something in banking."

She nodded. "Ashleigh said you met at the college."

"We did. Do you have a degree, Lauren?"

"No. I have some college credits but no degree."

"I don't suppose it's necessary since you already have a good job. You like working for the family business?"

Why did that question always seem to arise? "I do. My mom trained me to take over when she went back into real estate."

"How's that working for her? Her sales down?"

"Mom does well. She's been selling real estate for years. She's well-known in the community and gets lots of referrals."

"Definitely nice to have regular clientele."

Lauren could hear Ashleigh and the man she'd introduced as Seth Green getting acquainted in the backseat. "So how do you like our area?"

He glanced at her and said, "I really like it a lot. I enjoy the beach in particular."

"I rarely get to the beach," she admitted. "Between work and my other responsibilities I never have time. Jake and I went over to Carrot Island recently, but that's the first time in forever."

She noted that look again.

"I spend every Sunday at the beach."

"We went after church."

He didn't pursue her mention of church, and Lauren knew

he didn't attend. "What else do you like to do?"

"Hang out with friends. Sometimes we have pickup games at the apartment complex."

Everyone had friends.

He waited for a car that was leaving and angle-parked right in front of the restaurant. "Meant to be," he said with a big grin.

Austin's hand brushed her back now and again as the hostess led them to a private table in the front of the building. They placed their drink orders.

"Anyone interested in an appetizer?" the waitress asked. The men conferred over the menu and ordered wings and cheese fries.

"I'll be right back with your drinks."

"Hey, you can be the designated driver," Austin announced.

"Sorry. I don't drive." Lauren had chosen ice water. It struck her that it was a good thing her home was only blocks from the restaurant.

His head bobbed backward, and he looked at her with disbelief. "You don't drive? I don't think I ever knew anyone who didn't drive. Except for my grandmother."

Lauren knew she was a dinosaur in the modern world. She shrugged.

"I was going to ask what sort of car you drove."

So far he scored zero on the sensitivity scale. Lauren twisted uncomfortably in her chair. She glanced at Ashleigh who rolled her eyes.

"No car." She studied the menu.

"Do you know what you want for dinner?"

Lauren laid the menu on the table and rested her hands on top. "I'll have the Salad Sampler Trio."

"Sure that's going to be enough?" Austin asked. "You look like a girl with a hearty appetite."

Lauren couldn't help but feel insulted. "It's more than enough."

"Not that you're fat or anything."

His attempt to backpedal his way out didn't do much to soothe her ruffled feathers. "It's enough," she said succinctly.

"So what kind of music do you like?"

"Contemporary Christian. You?"

"Oh. I'm more into rock. Some rap. What about movies?"

Lauren unwrapped her silverware and laid it on the tabletop, pulling the napkin into her lap. "I suppose you'd call me a PG kind of girl."

With that, their conversation ground to a halt. Lauren supposed he was trying to come up with a topic. This wasn't going well. So far they had nothing in common.

The appetizer arrived. "Careful," the waitress warned as she slid the platters on the table. "Hot." She took the plates and more napkins from another waitress. Lauren took a couple of fries and a wing. "I love these," Ashleigh commented as she placed wings on her own plate.

Of course she did. Ashleigh was skinny.

Lauren wiped the sauce from her fingers and asked Seth, "What do you do?"

"I work for my dad. We have a furniture store. Green's Furniture."

Another longtime family business. "I know that store," Lauren said. "My mom has bought furniture there."

Austin waved his fork at Seth. "That's how we met. He sold me my recliner and my flat screen."

Seth grinned at Ashleigh and said, "I'm trying to get him to replace that pitiful excuse for a sofa."

"But he couldn't offer me as good a deal."

Ashleigh glanced at Lauren and said, "That sofa is the reason we never go to Austin's apartment. I'm pretty sure he sharpens those springs when no one is looking."

"What springs?" Seth joked. "Sit down on that thing and you'll never find your way back."

"Pretty heartless of you guys to demean my sofa like that,"

Austin declared with mock offense.

The couple laughed, and Lauren felt as though she were on the outside looking in. They lived in their own world and while she could possibly fit in, she didn't feel any strong desire to try.

"Yeah, Lauren, don't ever sit on his sofa," Ashleigh said. "Make him give you the recliner."

"Oh, I'll share with pleasure," Austin said with a grin that bordered on a leer. Why did she suspect that if he'd had a moustache he would have twirled the ends?

"I'll remember that." Not that there was any possibility she'd ever visit his apartment.

"After dinner, let's go back to my place and watch television. There's a game on tonight."

"No way," Ashleigh and Seth said together.

Austin fixed his puppy dog gaze on her. "What about you, Lauren? You interested in seeing my place?"

She looked at Ashleigh and the young woman answered for her, "We're not going back to your apartment."

"What did you plan to do after dinner?"

Go home, Lauren thought wistfully. She liked Austin okay but didn't feel the same connection she felt with Jake. She wasn't being fair. She'd known Jake longer.

"So, Lauren, why didn't you ever get your driver's license?"

"Austin! That's none of your business."

Ashleigh's angry outburst surprised them.

"I was making conversation," he defended.

"And if she'd wanted you to know she would have told you when you brought it up earlier."

Not wanting to cause controversy between the friends, Lauren said softly, "Health reasons."

Under lowered lashes, she watched him attempt to puzzle that one out.

"Do you run?"

She shook her head.

"I do five miles a day. My day stinks if I don't get my run in."
She tried to look impressed.

"I run all year long." He nodded toward his friends. "I tried
to get them to go with me, but they're not interested. What
about you, Lauren? You want to come along?"

She chuckled. "I wouldn't last through the first quarter
mile."

His eyes drifted over her again. "Wouldn't be long before
you could run a mile."

"I really don't have time, Austin. I'm usually at work by
seven and most days I don't get home until after seven in the
evening."

"Well, if you change your mind, give me a call. I'd love a
partner."

Their food arrived, and the conversation veered off to other
subjects the three of them had in common. Lauren listened,
wishing herself elsewhere.

"Anyone leave room for dessert?" the waitress asked.

They all groaned and shook their heads.

When their bill came, Austin pulled out a credit card and
slid it on the tray. Lauren felt she should pay her own way.
She hadn't been much of a date.

"Well, ladies, what would you like to do next?"

"Let's ride down to Atlantic Beach," Ashleigh suggested.
"That sound okay to you, Lauren?"

"Sounds great." They climbed into the vehicle and Lauren
reached for her seat belt. She fought the familiar feeling of
an attack as Austin backed out of the parking space.

He put the vehicle in drive and said, "That place has some
great food."

"It does."

She wanted to say more, but the movement of the car
added to her overwhelming sleepiness.

Lauren came out of the attack several minutes later with
Austin demanding, "What's wrong with her? Why did she

flake out like that?" There was laughter in his voice.

They were parked near the beach access.

"Shut up, Austin," Ashleigh snapped. She sat on the edge of the seat next to Lauren, holding her hand. "You okay?"

She managed a slight nod. Why had this happened tonight of all nights?

"Did she pass out?" Austin demanded from where he stood outside the passenger door.

In her head, Lauren could hear Jake urging her to share the truth. He didn't understand her narcolepsy was not something to be shared randomly. It required people who cared and wanted to help her, not those who would be turned off by her attacks.

"I'm sorry but I need to go home," she said, finding she couldn't open up to this man who stared at her with confusion in his brown gaze.

"Sure," Austin said.

He pulled up the seat for Ashleigh to clamber into the back. Lauren sensed Austin's gaze on her as they rode in silence. She wouldn't look at him. She could hear Ashleigh and Seth talking low in the back. Probably making plans to see each other again.

"I'll walk her inside," Ashleigh said as soon as Austin pulled into the driveway.

He made no effort to leave the car. Lauren opened the door and climbed out. She pulled the seat forward, and Ashleigh and Seth followed her from the car.

When Seth told Austin he'd catch a ride home with Ashleigh, Austin looked from one to the other, confused over the sudden change in plans.

Lauren leaned down and said, "I'm sorry about how the evening ended. I enjoyed meeting you." She rooted through her purse and pulled out a twenty. "Here. For my dinner."

He looked at the money and shook his head.

"No. I insist," Lauren said, pushing it into his hand. "It

hasn't been a very fun evening for you. There's time to watch your game or meet up with friends and do something fun."

Austin shrugged and took the money, dropping it on the console.

"It was nice meeting you, too, Lauren." The unhappiness in his expression told her he'd hoped for a different ending to his evening.

She smiled and waved good-bye before turning to go inside.

Ashleigh followed. "Are you okay?"

"I'm fine."

"Not your Mr. Right?" Ashleigh giggled and whispered, "I've known guys who put me to sleep, too."

"I feel bad."

Ashleigh shrugged. "He wasn't your type."

"Not sure I have a type but if I do, he wasn't the one. We didn't have much in common. But then I didn't give him much of a chance."

"It only takes seconds to form your first impression," Ashleigh reminded. "You knew from the moment you met whether things would click and they didn't."

"You and Seth really hit it off."

"He's so nice," she said dreamily.

Lauren nodded toward where Seth stood. "Go on. I'll see you Monday."

Ashleigh hugged her. "I'll find someone for you."

Lauren wanted to tell her not to bother. She'd already found someone, and he wasn't interested in anything but friendship. She had the feeling no one could ever measure up to Jake Greer. "Have fun." She called to Seth, "Nice meeting you."

"You, too."

She let herself into the house and found her parents and Jake sitting at the dining table. Teddy slept on the sofa.

"Back already?" her mother asked, looking dismayed.

"I had an attack when we got into the car after dinner.

I asked him to bring me home."

Jake looked past her. "And he didn't escort you inside?"

"Ashleigh walked me to the door. She and her date left in her car."

"So what happened to him?" Jake demanded.

"I suspect he's finding someone to help him complete his evening."

"Not your type?"

She shook her head. "We didn't have much in common."

Did he look pleased or was it her imagination? Jake wouldn't be happy about her failed attempt at making friends. Not after he'd encouraged her to get out and meet people. He'd think she hadn't tried hard enough.

"How was dinner?"

They talked about the restaurant, and Lauren refused dessert when her mother indicated the punch-bowl cake on the buffet. "Maybe later. I'm going to change."

She removed the new blouse and hung it in her closet, knowing she'd never wear it again without thinking of that failed first date. Lauren pulled on shorts and a T-shirt and dropped down onto her bed. She considered the way they had abandoned Austin and felt guilty.

There was a tap on the door. The door opened and her mom stuck her head inside. "You okay?"

"I don't feel good about the way the evening ended."

She came into the room. "Would you feel better if you'd stuck it out?"

Lauren shook her head. "He wasn't a Christian. Every time I mentioned God, he changed the subject."

"That is an important consideration. You need a man of faith. Love has its own problems, and your condition requires someone to stand by you in prayer when things get particularly difficult."

"I still feel bad," she said glumly. "I repaid him for my dinner. I thought that was fair."

"What happened?"

Lauren told her mother about their conversation. "We were going to ride down to Atlantic Beach. I woke up to find Ashleigh next to me and Austin asking what was going on. He laughed."

"You didn't tell him?"

She shook her head. "I can't tell everyone, Mom. Jake believes it would afford me more security, but I think information in the hands of the wrong people could be dangerous."

"I agree. There's no reason for everyone to know."

"But it seems unfair to pretend nothing happened. Maybe I should have explained."

"You think he would have asked you out again?"

Lauren pulled her leg under her on the bed. "Probably not. All I could think was this is not my crowd. I love Ashleigh, but I don't see me hanging out with her friends. They like to party and have fun."

"Most young people do, Laurie."

"But there's no way I'd put myself out there in the clubs."

"Did they lead you to believe that's where they hang out?"

"I think they party in each other's homes more. Not Austin's apartment, though. His furniture must consist of a really bad sofa, a recliner, and a big-screen television. He did say he was thinking of ordering a mattress from us. Guess I can forget that sale."

Her mother chuckled. "Your dad would probably furnish this place the same way if he didn't have me around." Suzanne took her daughter's hand. "Come on. I'm sure your dad has run out of conversation by now."

They settled in as if nothing had happened. Jake challenged Lauren to a game of Wii golf and the older Kingsleys joined in. Her parents had been surprised when Lauren gave them the game system for Christmas, but they played often. Her mother particularly enjoyed the fitness program.

They tried to keep their voices down as Teddy slept on the sofa. The four adults took turns and Lauren was the victor.

"See, Suzanne," her dad said. "I need to spend more time on the golf course."

"There's nothing stopping you, Greg. In fact, I suggest you get it out of your system while Jake is with us."

He frowned. "Let's don't talk about Jake leaving."

Lauren felt the same way. She knew their time together was growing shorter. It was already mid-September.

"This has been fun, but I need to get Teddy home to bed. I'll have those graphs for you on Monday."

The two men shook hands. Jake hugged Suzanne and then Lauren. "Want to go see the lighthouse tomorrow?"

Was he offering himself as a consolation prize? "It's supposed to be a nice day. I'll pick you up around eight and we could spend the day."

She nodded.

"Since we're going over to work in the attic, we could watch Teddy and Yapper for you," Suzanne volunteered. "I know Greg would be happy to have an excuse not to go up there."

"They'd probably be happier at home," Jake agreed.

"We'll see you in the morning then. We'll bring Lauren to your place."

thirteen

Over coffee early the following morning, Jake thought about Laurie's date. They hadn't clicked. Why exactly did that please him? Lauren needed someone who considered her special and would protect her from harm.

And that person couldn't be him. Right now, Teddy was as needy as he could handle. He'd learned his lesson with Gwen. No more women with unrealistic expectations.

Still, he hadn't liked that Austin guy. Everything about him had been too much. Too handsome. Too polished with the ladies. He wasn't her type. And the jerk hadn't even helped her to the door after she'd suffered the attack.

She deserved better. Much better. He filled the thermos with coffee and dumped snacks into the backpack he'd picked up last night.

Jake heard the Kingsleys' car pull up outside and opened the door. "Teddy's still asleep."

"Rough night?" Suzanne asked.

"I changed him into his pajamas and put him in the crib. He slept all night. You think something's wrong?"

"We all need more sleep at times. You two go ahead. We'll dress and feed him when he wakes."

Jake drove Down East toward Otway and Harkers Island and the Cape Lookout National Seashore. "Greg won't be much help with Teddy underfoot."

Lauren laughed. "Mom won't let Daddy near the attic."

"But she said. . ."

"He'd toss it all without a second thought. Mom has no intention of letting that happen."

Jake sighed almost dramatically. "That makes me feel better."

She smiled at him, and he suddenly felt wonderful.

They drove to the visitor center and went inside to study the displays, pick up literature, and watch a film entitled *Ribbon of Sand* before heading out to find a passenger transport ferry.

They parked and Jake carried the pack with their supplies. "Have we got everything?" he asked, glancing around. Lauren had the camera and binoculars. "I don't know how to act without Teddy."

"We could have brought him."

"He's happier at home. He's not a sun and sand fan."

They boarded the ferryboat, a flat-bottom skiff that would deliver them to the south-side beach. The captain welcomed them and told them where to sit. The other three passengers smiled at them. The ride across the open water was exhilarating, the spray splashing back on them now and then.

They wore jeans and carried lightweight jackets to ward off the chill, though the sun seemed determined to handle the task alone.

When they arrived at the island, the captain advised everyone of the pickup time. Jake clambered off the boat and offered his hand. Awareness shot through him as Lauren took it.

"There you go," Lauren said, pointing to the Cape Lookout Lighthouse. "Built one hundred and fifty years ago to help mariners safely negotiate the dreaded Lookout Shoals, aka Graveyard of the Atlantic."

"I heard the locals call it the Diamond Lady."

Lauren nodded. "The painted diamond pattern aids in direction, black north-south, and white east-west. One hundred sixty-three feet tall with two hundred and one steps and a three-hundred-sixty-degree view of the Crystal Coast from the observation deck."

"Can we climb it today?"

She shook her head. "Season is mid-May through mid-September."

Jake sighed. "I meant to come sooner."

They toured the area, Jake taking photos of her in front of the lighthouse and her doing the same for him. And he handed over the camera when another couple offered to take one of them together. They also saw the Keeper's House and the former U.S. Coast Guard Station.

Later they boarded the skiff again and went to Shackelford Banks to see the wild Banker ponies. The free-roaming Spanish horses were said to have descended from horses that swam to the island four hundred years before.

They had quite a walk before they located a group of horses. They kept their distance as Jake raised the camera and snapped a number of photos.

Lauren sat reading the flyer she'd picked up from the park service. "They divide themselves into harems and bachelor bands. Each dominant alpha stallion guards a harem of mares and foals. Sometime between a year and a half to five years the young fillies and colts leave the harem. The females join other harems and the males form loose bachelor bands." She laughed outright at that. "Bachelor band life gives the colts a chance to spar and mature into stallions so they can challenge the existing alphas."

Just like human bachelors, Jake thought.

"You want to go shell hunting?"

He brushed sand from her arm. "I'll pass. I don't need shells to remember this day."

Her gaze met his as she said, "Me neither."

❧

After that day, life shifted into high speed. The days disappeared as September slipped into October and all too soon Thanksgiving loomed in the very near future.

"What are your plans for the holiday?" Lauren asked Jake over lunch in the cafeteria.

"We're going to Arizona to see Teddy's grandparents. I promised I'd bring him, but I've been so tied up that we haven't seen them since July. Afterward, we'll go to my brother's home in California for Thanksgiving."

Lauren frowned, feeling suddenly sad. "You'll be gone for Teddy's birthday."

He nodded. "That's why we have to go. They insist on spending his first birthday with Teddy."

She would have loved throwing a party for Teddy, but it was only right that he be with his grandparents. "What about Christmas?"

Jake shook his head. "It's too soon to go back. We'll do our celebrating over Thanksgiving and come back here to finish up the contract."

Lauren refused to think about them leaving forever. "Did you see the article in Sunday's paper?"

"I did. Great job," he enthused. "Nice photo of you and your dad. How did you get Greg to participate?"

Lauren grinned. "Mom laid out his best suit that morning, knowing the reporter and photographer would be here. And then I dropped in with them and he had to talk."

"Any feedback yet?"

"I haven't checked with sales."

"I see they have the television program playing in the sales area."

She grimaced. "I think Daddy might be behind that. Though he's not admitting to anything."

"Of course not." Jake enjoyed this playful side of father and daughter. "You have time to sit in on an employee meeting this afternoon?"

Lauren shook her head regretfully. "Doctor's appointment."

"Can you reschedule?"

Though tempted, she needed to get her blood test results. "I've put it off too long already."

"I'll ask Greg to sit in."

"Don't let him make any promises he can't keep."

"He understands he can't be so generous and stay in business."

She sipped from her water bottle and returned it to the table. "I hate that for him. He gets such joy from doing for others, but he's got to draw the line somewhere."

Jake stood and gathered his tray. "I'm out of here. Hey, Laurie," he said, pausing next to the table. "Want to go Christmas shopping with me?"

"Won't hurt to get a head start now that I have a few more people on my list."

He groaned. "Please don't buy a lot of stuff for Teddy, or I'll have to hire a moving company."

She shook her head. "You can get your things in a U-Haul trailer."

"Nah, we'll need a truck. I'm buying mattresses and Teddy needs his bed, too."

That made her smile. "As fast as he's growing you can invest in a twin mattress for Teddy. For that matter, we'll give you the company discount for everyone on your Christmas list."

"Imagine wrapping that kind of present," Jake said with a shake of his head.

&

Later that afternoon Jake walked down the hall with Greg Kingsley.

"That went well," Greg offered, apparently pleased with the meeting outcome.

"It did. Making them aware they'll benefit as the company benefits is good. I think they'll be inspired by the improved bonus plan. Every person in that room knows people who need new bedding."

Jake studied the man who had brought him there. "Greg, you know I'm close to accomplishing what you set out for me to do. Our contract is up in January, and I'm sending out proposals for my next job."

"You don't have to go. I've been thinking, and you could make a big difference here at Sleep Dreams. I'm not getting any younger, and Lauren can't handle it alone. She does a great job, but the stress would be too much for her. I'd like to reduce my hours and spend more time with Suzanne. Maybe travel a bit."

"You'd leave Lauren alone?"

Greg hesitated and said, "If she had someone to call on when she needed help."

Jake felt the pressure building in the back of his head and reached to massage his neck. "I can't do it, Greg."

"Can't or won't?"

"I'm a problem solver. You no longer have a problem."

"I wouldn't say that."

"Laurie's doing well."

"I worry about her. Who will take care of my little girl when I'm no longer around?"

A huge knot formed in Jake's throat. He felt Greg's pain, understood his fear. "She's not a little girl, Greg. She's a woman who can handle what life throws at her. She will take care of herself. Laurie wants you and Suzanne to enjoy your lives. You should do those things you mentioned. She can handle things here."

Greg Kingsley looked resigned. "We've lived with this for so long. It's changed our lives."

"Lauren won't give up. You and Suzanne taught her that."

"Suzanne did all the hard work. I kept this place going and provided the money."

"That's important, too, Greg. Don't ever doubt the role you play in your daughter's life. She loves you very much."

"We keep praying research will find the cure."

"Strides are being made in medicine every day."

"She's going to miss you and Teddy. We all will."

"We'll miss you, too, Greg. Our time here has been great, but it's time for us to move on. You could always hire a manager to help Laurie. She would look after your interests."

"If you change your mind, you're always welcome here."

Jake detected a slump to the man's shoulders. He made his

way back to his office, thinking of the offer and what it could mean to him and Teddy. A long-term position would require him to settle down and would give Teddy a home. Stability. If he were listing positives and negatives, there would be a lot of positives.

But what about Laurie? He didn't want to put her in the negative column, but Jake knew that's where she'd end up if she got involved with him. Gwen had told him he was a terrible husband often enough that Jake knew she was right. Laurie didn't need a selfish man in her life.

❧

Lauren flipped the page in her calendar book. Five days since Jake and Teddy left for Arizona. She fingered Yapper's ears. "You miss them, too, don't you?"

When Jake asked if she'd mind checking on Yapper, Lauren suggested the dog would be lonely without them and it would be easier if she were at their house.

"Gerry said she'd keep her, but she's going to visit her kids for Thanksgiving," Jake said.

"Good for her. I don't think she's ever left Beaufort."

"The kids can't come and she wants to be with them. Are you sure Yapper's no problem?"

"She will be fine with us. Yapper and Fred get along great."

Jake sighed with regret. "Seems senseless to take time now when we'll be wrapping up the contract in a few weeks."

Lauren ignored the obvious. "I'm sure your family wants to see you before then."

"It's not that long before we leave, Laurie."

"But it's not now," she offered resolutely. "You'll be back for Christmas and the New Year."

Lauren found herself holding on to that fact, wishing it could be longer. She was determined to make the best of their last days together. She'd deal with the fallout after they left. Hopefully she could fight back the depression that she felt building about the edges of her life.

fourteen

Jake and Teddy returned, and they worked and played together and prepared to celebrate Jesus' birthday.

When Jake said he didn't plan to have a tree, Lauren felt bad for Teddy and urged him to reconsider. She and her mother insisted he needed to celebrate the holiday for his son's sake. They shopped for the tree and decorations and even picked up stockings for the mantel.

Tonight she'd come home with him after work to decorate. He looked on with doubt. "I don't know who will tear it down first—Teddy or Yapper."

Lauren thought she detected a mischievous glint in the little boy's eyes as he toddled among the decorations in the room. No doubt he couldn't wait to get his hands on the tree.

"I should have a tabletop tree."

She shook her head. "No. This is better. We'll secure it to the wall so Teddy doesn't pull it over on himself."

"What about the ornaments? He could get cut."

As if to prove a point, Teddy pulled a box from the coffee table. The ornaments rolled about the floor, still intact. Teddy picked up a bright red ornament and offered it to her.

Lauren tapped on it. "That's why I bought the non-breakable kind."

Jake looped an arm about her shoulder and pulled her close. "You're so smart."

She grinned. "I know. We need to finish up. Mom said she'd pick me up around eight."

"I could have taken you home."

"No sense in taking Teddy out into the cold."

The weather had turned unseasonably cold for the past

144

few days, and she didn't want to risk him getting sick.

Soon the tree lights winked at them with beautiful abandon among the mixture of children's ornaments they had chosen and the plastic candy garland.

"Teddy will try to eat this," Jake told her as he fingered the candy garland.

"Stop being such a Scrooge."

Lauren went to hang the wreath on the front door. She'd placed electric candles in the windows earlier. Back inside, she draped garland over the mantel and added red bows. "I love Christmas."

"I saw."

She looked at him and laughed. The Kingsley family had decorated their home the previous weekend, and he'd showed up at one point when it looked like an explosion in a Christmas factory.

"It came out beautifully," Jake said.

Lauren opened the box they had picked up earlier and studied the memory quilt. "Isn't it beautiful?" she asked, running her fingers over the bits of fabric that had been her grandmother's.

"Your mom will love it."

"It's going to make her cry." Lauren knew her mother would treasure the quilt but hated the thought of making her sad. "The Christmas cantata is this Sunday night. Are you going?"

Jake grumbled as he sorted tangled ornament hooks. He pulled out two and hung ornaments on the tree. "Yes. I finished my shopping over the weekend. Had some wrapped in the stores and bought bags and tissue paper for the rest."

At least he wasn't shopping at the convenience store on Christmas Eve, Lauren thought.

"Don't forget the company Christmas party is Friday night. We distributed the longevity checks at the end of November."

Jake looked perplexed. "I thought you intended to give them a cost of living raise instead."

"Daddy ran the numbers and says we can do both."

"Lauren. . ."

She held up a hand. "I know, Jake. Daddy's not going to relent. He wants them to have this, and you're not going to change his mind. I will say they've brought in a number of new customers lately. We've issued a lot of bonus checks for referrals. Ashleigh even sold a mattress to Austin Danforth."

Lauren enjoyed the holidays more than she had in years. Jake and Teddy joined their family for dinner, and the future was forgotten as they concentrated on Christmas Day. Her mother adored the quilt and became quite emotional when she saw what Lauren had done.

A surprise snowstorm the day after Christmas forced them to close shop for the day. Lauren sat in the window seat, watching the snow fall and wondering what Jake and Teddy were doing. She wondered if they were out playing in the snow. Wished she were there with them. Around two, she checked her e-mail and found a photo of Teddy with a child-sized snowman next to a man-sized one. "Wish you were here," she read.

Her parents held their annual New Year's Eve party and Jake and Teddy attended. The toddler slept on the daybed in the guest room as they rang in the New Year together.

As she marked the days off on her calendar, Lauren thought about what would happen soon.

Yet no matter how often she told herself to stop wishing for the impossible, the hope refused to be stayed. Her dad had said he offered Jake a long-term job. Maybe he'd change his mind and decide to stay.

They spent the workdays wrapping up, discussing the process, finalizing plans for how they would continue. Every night, she came home tired and feeling as though her heart would break. Then three weeks later they were saying good-bye to Jake and Teddy. The going-away party was held in the company cafeteria. Jake had made a big impression on their workers, and they showed up in force to wish him well for the future. He held Teddy in one arm and shook hands with the other.

"I'm going to miss you so much," Lauren said when her turn came, cradling Teddy's cheeks in her hands as she kissed his forehead.

"We'll miss you, too." Jake boosted his son with his arm. "He's become attached to your family and Gerry. He's not going to understand."

Lauren took Teddy and cuddled him close. She looked up at Jake. "Promise you'll come back for a visit."

"You know how it is, Laurie. I promise with good intentions, but life gets hectic and we never make it back. You see how it is with my parents and in-laws."

She did understand. People came and went in her life and while she was blessed for knowing them, the good ones were very much missed.

"There's something else," Jake began almost tentatively. "Say no if you want, but I feel it's the best thing for all involved. Would you be willing to take Yapper?"

Lauren's mouth dropped open.

"Teddy's too young to have a pet," Jake said. "And now that he's walking, poor Yapper spends all her time looking for places to hide."

"But you'd. . ."

"We would miss her, but I'm terrified she's not going to survive Teddy. I cringe every time he gets her in his clutches. I try to make him understand, but he drags her around like one of his stuffed animals."

She knew Jake was right. Yapper would be no competition for the toddler's affections. "You know I love Yapper."

"Then she's yours. I feel better knowing she will be with someone I trust and she'll be happier, too. If I were fair,

I'd find a permanent home for Teddy, but I can't leave him behind."

"No. Don't do that." She visualized Teddy when he started his *dadadada* chant the moment he laid eyes on Jake. "He needs you. Have you considered finding a job that keeps you in one place?"

"I'm good at troubleshooting, Laurie. I enjoy change."

She looked him in the eye and said, "You're good at a lot of things. You'd find a challenge in any job you took on."

Later that afternoon, Lauren hid her tears as she waved them off.

He'd turned back to her after placing Teddy in his car seat in the cab of the large rental truck and pulled her into a hug. "You're a special person, Laurie. Promise me you'll never forget that. And that you'll keep trying to do those things you dream of doing."

She nodded. The way he'd touched her heart in these months was not something she could easily forget. He and Teddy had given her so much, helped her understand how narrow her world was without love. She could have friends who were trustworthy and understood what she was going through. The parameters of her almost solitary world had changed thanks to Jake and she had to be thankful. "I can't thank you enough for all you've done."

He stared at her for several seconds and then kissed her gently before turning away to climb into the rental truck.

Her hand came over her mouth, holding back the sobs. She'd known saying good-bye would hurt. Jake had made a major difference in her life. He awakened her to life's possibilities, and for that she'd always be thankful.

She stood in the parking lot, staring after the rental truck long after it disappeared in the distance.

"You okay, Laurie?" Her mother's arm curved about her waist, comforting her in the way only her mother could.

"I'm going to miss them."

"We all will. They made quite an impact on our family."

Lauren nodded, swiping away the tear that spilled down her cheek. "I owe him, Mom. Jake changed my world."

"Do you love him?"

She met her mother's gaze and nodded. They shared too much history for her not to tell the truth.

"Does he know?"

Lauren suspected that deep down inside Jake did know, but not because she'd voiced her feelings or tried to change his mind. "I wouldn't do that to him."

"What do you mean wouldn't?"

"I'm not the woman for him. I can't give Jake what he needs."

"I'm not so sure Jake knows what he needs. I suspect he's running from his past."

Lauren's gaze jerked up to her mother's face. "Why do you think that?"

"Why would he want a transient lifestyle, particularly with a small child? Most men are ready to settle down at his age. I hope he realizes Teddy needs permanence in his life soon."

"Jake provides permanence."

Suzanne's head moved slowly from side to side. "Too many people coming and going in Teddy's world. Eventually he'll stop bonding for fear everyone he loves will leave."

"Do you think Jake knows that?"

Her mother shrugged. "He's Teddy's father. I'm praying for God to open his eyes. Teddy has already lost too many people in his young life." Suzanne touched her cheek gently. "I'm praying for you, honey. God will get you through this."

Lauren reached up to squeeze her hand. "He always has. I'd better get back to work."

"Why don't we go out to dinner tonight? Take our minds off this."

She wasn't in the mood. "You and Daddy go."

"No. I'll fix something at home."

"See you later."

Dinner that night was a solemn affair. They ate in silence and worked together to clear the table. Her mother had made an extra effort with the meal, but the events of the day stole their appetites.

The glasses clinked together as her mother picked them up and headed for the sink. "Laurie, do you still want your own place?"

Did she? She hadn't given the idea much thought lately.

"I was thinking. Now that Jake's gone, you could move into Mom's place."

She couldn't. There were too many memories of Jake and Teddy there. She couldn't live with a constant reminder of their absence.

"Laurie?"

She shook her head quickly. "I don't want to move. Not now."

"That's fine, sweetie," her mother said. "You can stay right here for as long as you like."

Lauren had professed to desire a change in her life. With Jake by her side, that had been easy to consider. Without him, she couldn't imagine how she would survive, much less make major changes in the life she'd always known.

A box arrived a few days later, and Lauren smiled when she opened it to find piles of little doggie outfits. She read the note Jake had included, "Checked the weather and thought Yapper might appreciate these."

The new year continued. As she'd known it would, the depression hit her head-on like an eighteen-wheeler running over a subcompact. Despite taking her medication, Lauren suffered more frequent attacks.

Ashleigh came up with another blind date, but Lauren refused. "I won't do that to someone else. I'm not what your friend is looking for."

"You don't know that. This guy's ready to settle down. He's

not into partying or chasing women. He's a one-woman kind of guy. It's Seth's older brother, Chase."

She glanced at her assistant. She knew Ashleigh and Seth had been a couple for months now and she had admitted to her hope that he would ask her to marry him. "Has he proposed yet?"

Ashleigh shook her head and sighed. "No, not yet. Chase retired from the military and came home to join the family business." Then she frowned. "Though he's nearly forty."

Ancient to this younger woman, Lauren thought. "I appreciate you thinking of me, but things aren't going well right now. I'm having attacks all the time, and I'm afraid if I don't get my life back to some semblance of normalcy, it's only going to get worse."

Concern filled her assistant's expression. "Is there anything I can do?"

"Be my friend and pray for me," Lauren told her.

"I am your friend, but I'm not so sure about the praying part."

Lauren knew that some people would feel her next question a violation of their rights, but as Ashleigh's friend she needed to ask. "Do you know Christ as your Savior?"

"We weren't a church family."

"Jesus loves you, Ashleigh. If you'd like to talk or even go to church with us, let me know."

The young woman nodded. "If you'll sign these, I'll get them in the mail this afternoon."

Lauren wrote her name with a flourish and handed over the letters.

&

Jake glanced down at Teddy. "Ready for lunch, buddy?"

"Lunch." His son's vocabulary was growing.

In the days since he'd been back at his apartment, he'd sent out more proposals but had no responses. What was going on? Why the delay? He'd worked steadily since he'd gotten his degree and now it seemed no one wanted him. Businesses were in trouble. The economy was bad. Why wasn't anyone calling?

He should have stayed at Sleep Dreams. No, he'd been right in moving on. It wasn't right to take the Kingsleys' money when he'd done what they'd hired him to do.

Almost as if he read his mind, Teddy looked at Jake and chanted, "Laurie."

Jake had heard it several times a day since they'd left North Carolina. He shifted his son to his lap and said, "Yeah, buddy, I miss her, too."

He missed her bright smile when he walked into the room, her teasing and funny little jokes. The way she played with Teddy and Yapper. He even missed Yapper.

"Want Laurie, Daddy?" Teddy's little forehead wrinkled.

"Sure, why not." Jake reached for the cell phone on the table and dialed Lauren's office number. It was after lunch there. She'd be at her desk this time of day.

It rang four times before her voice mail picked up. He listened to the message. Weird. He hit the one and listened again. "You've reached the office of Lauren Kingsley. I am temporarily out of the office. If you have concerns that require immediate attention, please hang up and call. . ." He recognized Ashleigh's extension.

Jake disconnected and shifted straighter in the chair before dialing Greg's private number. The man sounded harried.

"Greg, Jake here. Where's Laurie? I got her voice mail."

"Oh, Jake, it's terrible. She fell last Tuesday after work. Broke both her wrists."

Stunned, he demanded, "What's going on? I thought she had her narcolepsy under control."

"She's been having problems," Greg admitted. "Laurie's really struggling with the attacks right now."

Not what he wanted to hear. "Both wrists?"

"Yeah. She wanted to go into a rehab center until the casts

come off. Suzanne refused. Laurie's not doing well."

"I'm sorry. Is there anything I can do?"

Greg paused and then he said, "Maybe a call would brighten her spirits. Her mother and I haven't been able to help much in that area."

"I'm sure that's not true," Jake discounted. "She's depressed because she hurt herself so badly."

"I don't understand why it was so bad this time. She's had more than her share of bumps and bruises. Laurie's fallen over on her head a time or two and on the street, but she usually crumples into a heap. This time she pitched over the parking barrier."

"Teddy was chanting her name today and I thought I'd call so she could hear. I'll give her a call at the house. Can she answer the phone?"

"She has a speaker phone in her room. I think Suzanne had a client this morning so Lauren's probably still in bed. Her mother doesn't want her wandering about while she's casted. She's afraid Laurie will suffer an attack and hurt herself worse."

"I'll call her now."

She sounded far from her usual happy self when she said hello.

"Laurie? It's Jake. I spoke to your dad. He told me you'd hurt yourself."

"Jake?" she repeated almost in disbelief.

"Yeah. Teddy was calling for you. I had no idea."

"How is Teddy?" Her voice grew softer with the question.

"He's okay. We're at our apartment."

"You don't have a job?"

"Not yet. It's the first time I've been out of work since college."

Teddy burbled, "Laurie, hi."

Jake tilted the phone so she could hear.

"Hey, buddy."

Jake chuckled as he fought the baby for the phone. "He's bouncing up and down and trying to take the phone from me."

"I miss you, Teddy. Yapper misses you, too."

"Where Yap?"

"He's developed quite a vocabulary."

"Mostly no and the names of his favorite people. So how are you managing?"

"Not very well. I can't do anything for myself. Mom and Dad feed me, and I have an aide who comes in to help me bathe and dress."

She sounded near tears.

"What happened? Did you have an attack?"

"I wasn't paying attention and tripped."

"Is there anything I can do?"

"Pray. I'm glad you called. It's good hearing from you."

They talked for several minutes, catching up on the time they'd been apart.

"The trip went okay, but I don't think I want to drive pulling a vehicle too often."

"I still say you could have gotten the stuff in a trailer if you'd dismantled the crib."

"Nothing ever goes back together the same way. I lugged the mattress upstairs to my bedroom and put the rest in storage in my uncle's garage. Don't tell your mom, but Teddy and I are sleeping together. There's nowhere in this apartment for his crib."

"Maybe you should have kept your house."

"Too many memories and a waste when you consider how little time I spent at home." There was a pause, and Jake wondered if something had happened.

"What about Teddy?" she asked finally. "Don't you worry that he won't become attached to people if he's always on the move?"

He did worry about separating his son from the people he loved, but what choice did he have? "I'm not going anywhere.

Teddy will always have me."

At least Jake hoped that would be the case.

Life didn't come with guarantees. Accidents and sickness took loved ones every day. Jake often thought about what would happen to Teddy in the event either of those affected their lives. His mother was growing older, and he wasn't so sure his stepfather would welcome a child in their home. Gwen's parents would take him, but they were getting on in years. He supposed he could trust his brother to take care of Teddy, but he didn't like thinking about it. Too morbid.

"Tell me what to send to cheer you up."

"Short of a miracle cure, prayers and the occasional phone call would be most appreciated. Poor Mom is picking up my slack at the office as well as handling her own work and taking care of me. I feel so bad about putting more on her. I'm trying to fade into the background and not complain. Ashleigh's been a great help. She's taken on a number of things I usually handle and doing a great job."

"How are the attacks?"

Her pause gave him the answer.

"They're worse. My medications are off schedule. When Mom's not here, I can't open the bottles. Forget childproof caps. Mine are cast-proof."

"Why don't you ask your mom. . ."

"She already has too much to do. I'm stuck here in bed anyway, so what does it matter if I have an attack." The self-disgust in her tone was palpable.

"Laurie, I'm so sorry this happened to you."

"I wouldn't wish it on my worst enemy."

"Like you'd have one." Teddy started to whine. "It's time for his lunch."

"No peas and carrots for my buddy."

"Call me if you want to talk."

She sighed and he said, "You can't push the buttons."

"I'll have mom put you on speed dial."

Teddy started to wail.

"You'd better go. Thanks for calling, Jake. I'm glad you did. Kiss Teddy for me."

&

He kissed the top of his son's head and said, "Laurie's hurting bad, Teddy."

"See Laurie?" His son appeared puzzled as he looked around the room for her.

"Yes, Laurie," he said, bouncing Teddy on his knee as he allowed his thoughts to drift. How terrible it must be to have both hands in casts. He wished he were there to help her.

What if he went back to Beaufort? What could he do? Put her in a chair next to Teddy and shovel food into both their mouths? Lauren had more adult needs.

He thought of the pain in her voice when she spoke of the burden she'd placed on her mother. At one time, he'd suggested her parents were overprotective, but he now understood they were motivated by love for their child. It didn't matter how old she was. Lauren needed them and they'd be there for her always.

Jake considered how much of her pain he'd caused with his crusade to convince her she needed to change. He carried his son into the kitchen. The back door opened to admit his mother, who had been shopping.

"Hey, Mom. I didn't expect you back so soon."

Stella Greer Simmons piled the bags on the counter. "I gave up. Couldn't find anything that appealed." She reached for her grandson and nodded toward the bags. "I picked up the food and diapers you had on the grocery list."

Jake frowned. "You didn't have to do that. I planned to go out later."

"Now you don't have to. Want me to feed him his lunch?"

"I can do it."

She hugged Teddy close. "Go do something else. I want to spend quality time with my grandson."

She'd been like this ever since she arrived Sunday afternoon, taking over Teddy's care every chance she got. She'd insisted she needed a grandbaby fix, and he hadn't argued. Except for their brief visit at Thanksgiving, it had been months since she'd seen her grandson.

Jake used the time to follow up on job leads. He pulled out his laptop and checked his e-mail. Nothing. Why wasn't anyone responding to his proposals? Sure, it hadn't been that long, but he usually had a job waiting when he wrapped up the previous one.

He typed in the link for Sleep Dreams website. Lauren had gotten the site redone and it looked great. He considered her reluctance to take over certain tasks and to be in the limelight, but whatever she did she did well. She'd carried out every plan he'd outlined.

Jake searched online for a local florist. He placed an order for a rainbow bouquet of roses, hoping their beauty would boost Laurie's spirits.

After a while, he went back into the living room. Teddy toddled about the room, chasing his ball, and his grandmother's gaze followed him.

An afternoon talk show played on the television. Jake sat down next to his mother. He watched for a few minutes before he asked, "How can you watch this stuff?"

"You should pay attention. You might learn something."

He doubted that. Jake reached for the magazine he'd placed on the coffee table earlier and thumbed through the pages. He couldn't tune out the woman on the television as she talked about her failed marriage.

"He expected me to ignore my needs and focus on his. He could be so selfish. After a while, I hated him."

"Their marriage was probably already in trouble," he muttered.

His mother glanced at him and said, "A man can't expect a woman to give up everything and be happy with love. It doesn't work that way."

"We don't expect that."

She flashed him a pitying look.

Teddy came over and patted his tiny hands against Jake's legs. "Play, Daddy?"

He swung him up and caught him. "Hey, buddy."

Teddy stood with his bare feet planted against his father's chest, holding on to his fingers as tightly as possible. His son offered him a grin. Jake looked on with pride. "You are something else, Teddy Greer."

The television program served as white noise for his thoughts as he held his son. In the months since Gwen's death, he'd become attached to Teddy to a degree he'd never imagined possible. Would that have happened if she hadn't died? Or would they have eventually gone their separate ways, citing irreconcilable differences? Would he have lost this opportunity to bond with his son like this? Jake feared the latter might have been the case.

"Mom, if you fell in love with someone who had a serious medical problem, would you stay?"

Recognizing his need to talk, she used the remote to lower the volume. "You spoke the vows yourself, Jake. In sickness and health. Once said, they were a vow to God as well as your wife."

"No. I mean before proposals and marriage. In the getting-to-know-each-other/dating stage. Would you walk away?"

She looked puzzled. "How could you walk away from love?"

Jake thought maybe that was exactly what he'd done. "I met this woman in North Carolina. Her name is Lauren. She has narcolepsy."

He shared how the disorder affected her life, talked about his erroneous accusation, how he'd encouraged her to reach for the things she wanted in life, and even how happy he'd been when her blind date had been unsuccessful.

"Teddy liked her from day one, but she wouldn't hold him

out of fear that he could be hurt. By the time we left, she and Teddy were very comfortable together."

"She's the Laurie he calls for?"

Jake nodded. He'd thought Teddy would forget in time, but he hadn't.

"What does this problem mean to you as a couple?"

"When she takes her medication regularly, Laurie functions fine. She's a CFO for the company and has a wonderful support base in her parents. At first, I thought they were overprotective and urged her to become more independent, but now I realize they're a team. They work together to keep Lauren's life from being unbearable. But she still has the attacks, trusts very few people, and lives in fear of strangers."

"Seems she's won your heart. What will you do?"

Jake sighed heavily. "She's very easy to love. But I vowed no more helpless women."

His mother's eyes widened. "You saw Gwen as helpless? I always admired her strength."

Shocked, he repeated, "Strength?"

Stella shrugged. "I couldn't have done what Gwen did. She was alone in that big house with a baby and a tiny dog."

"I had to work to support my family," Jake said. "I couldn't be at her beck and call. She knew how things would be when we married, but that didn't keep her from nagging me at every opportunity."

"Perhaps her needs changed as she matured," his mother suggested. "She needed her husband around more often. We marry for companionship, Jake."

"At first, I asked her to travel with me, but she refused. Then she had Teddy and Yapper and her family."

"But you weren't there, Jake. Husbands fill a special place in a woman's heart. We need you more than you realize, and it's not all about the honey-do list. I think you have some praying to do. Ask yourself if you're man enough to take Lauren on."

Her comment pricked his masculinity. "What do you mean 'man enough'?"

"You have to be sure this is what you want. You can't decide it's too hard and walk away later."

"I wouldn't do that to her," he muttered.

Teddy worked his way across the sofa into his grandmother's arms. She pulled him close. "I would hope not. I raised you better than that. You need to seek God's plan in all this. Would she be able to give you more children?"

He lifted one shoulder. "She wants a family but worries about caring for them. We would need help. I had this great woman caring for Teddy and Yapper while we were there."

"If it's right, you'll make it work."

"Is it too soon?" he asked. "It's barely been a year since Gwen died."

"That's a personal choice, Jake. You'll know when you're ready to marry again."

That night, he lay on the sofa, his back hurting as his mom and Teddy shared his comfortable bed.

Though he tried to convince himself differently, Jake realized that in a way he'd expected Gwen to sublimate her needs for his. And then he'd gotten angry when she wouldn't. Couldn't. She wasn't nagging. She was asking for what she needed from him.

And his way of dealing with it had been to stay away even longer periods of time. He expected the house, a dog, and Teddy to be enough for her. His mom was right. She'd married a man, expecting him to keep the vows he'd spoken on their wedding day.

He could tell himself he'd done it for Gwen, but Jake knew he'd been selfish. He hadn't cheated on his wife, but he'd lived like a bachelor. He stayed in hotels, ate out, watched sports, and did his own thing until guilt forced him back home to his role of husband and father.

Then after a few days, when he decided he couldn't bear

another minute of the arguing, he'd pack up and take off for the next adventure, leaving her behind to hold down the home front until he returned.

Gwen hadn't planned on a solo marriage, but that's what she'd gotten. He'd been the selfish one. Putting his needs first and expecting her to pretend everything was wonderful.

What had Lauren said today? Something about Teddy not bonding with people. Would Teddy suffer from disassociation because of him? No, Jake decided. That wouldn't happen.

"Lord," he called softly, "please tell me what You would have me do. Should I pluck Lauren from her safe haven and take her away to a new environment that would be alien to everything she knows? Would my love for her be enough? Does she love me? Is she the one You intend for me?

"Teddy and I need love in our lives, and You provided us with such a wonderful loving group of people while we were in Beaufort that we're spoiled. Take care of her, Lord. Heal her hands as quickly as possible so that she can have her life back. Help her get her medications back on schedule so the attacks occur less frequently.

"And as always, Lord, thank You for Your love and grace. Without You, I am nothing."

Only God knows the answer, Jake thought as he concluded his prayer. He tossed and turned for another hour before falling asleep. He dreamed of Lauren and her broken wrists.

"You're up early," his mother said the next morning when he came into the kitchen.

"Tough night."

"You want coffee?"

He nodded, and she poured the fresh brew into a mug and set it on the table before him. "Breakfast?"

Jake grimaced and said no. He reached for the cup and took several fortifying gulps before he spoke again.

"I'm going back to North Carolina. Greg Kingsley offered

me a job managing the company."

"Is this what you want or are you nervous about not hearing back from the RFPs?"

"It's about Lauren. And the life I hope we can share."

"So you made a decision?"

"I did as you suggested and prayed over the matter. Then I tossed and turned until everything came clear."

"So she's worth the effort?"

"The boss's daughter," he offered with a wry smile. "I said I would never do that again, but we plan and God laughs."

Stella smiled. "But what sort of wife will she be?"

"I don't even know that she'd consider marrying me," Jake admitted. "But I feel strongly enough for her that I'm willing to help take care of her now and hope for a future."

"What about dependent women?"

"I wasn't fair to Gwen, Mom. I loved her and I don't regret marrying her, but I never explained what our lives would be like. I expected her to accept my plan without complaint. We both suffered as a result of my immaturity. That won't happen again. Besides, Teddy needs a stable home and people who love him as much as he loves them. People who won't disappear from his life every few months."

"What do you need?"

"A woman who loves me."

"When are you going?"

"After your visit. Will you come see us in North Carolina?"

"You know I will."

He nodded satisfaction with the plan that had suddenly come clear to him. "You'll like the area." He rubbed his bristly cheeks. "I'll shower and shave. How about two of your favorite guys taking you out to lunch?"

"I'd love that."

His mother stayed the remainder of her two weeks and during that time Jake spoke to Lauren several times. She'd loved the flowers and seemed cheered by their chats. He longed to be closer to her.

Laurie told him she felt more useful when her mother brought work home for her to complete.

"She says she doesn't remember how to do some of it," Lauren told Jake. "I suppose things have changed. Feels good to do something besides feel sorry for myself."

He called Greg Kingsley the day after his mom left for home. "Hello, Greg."

"Jake," he called, sounding happy to hear from him. "How are you? And Teddy?"

"We're fine. Mom left for home yesterday, and we're getting used to not having her around to spoil us. And I'm glad to get my bed back."

Greg chuckled. "Laurie's doing better. I didn't realize how much she does around here. Suze is serving as Lauren's hands, and they're working together to handle the office paperwork."

"I talked to her earlier. She's happy to have something to occupy her time."

"What's on your mind? I know you didn't call to check on Laurie since you've already talked to her."

"I wanted to ask if the management offer is still on the table."

"You thinking of coming back?"

"I've been praying about my life, and it seems God is leading me home."

"I think you'll be a fine addition to the Sleep Dreams family."

Maybe even the Kingsley family. Jake didn't talk about his feelings to her father. He needed to talk to Laurie first.

"When should we expect you?"

"I'll get things in order here and hopefully be back there in two weeks. Will you ask Suzanne if the house is still available? Should we tell Laurie or keep it a surprise?" He paused and then answered his own question. "We should tell her. A surprise might bring on an attack."

"You know, Jake, if I had any doubts, that comment pretty much reassured me that you'll be good for Laurie. You care about her, and that's the most important thing in the world to her mother and me."

"We miss her."

"Come home, Jake."

fifteen

And home was exactly the way it felt, Jake thought as he walked through the front door of the little house. He'd missed the place. His apartment lacked the same feel.

He'd called Gerry Hart, and she was ready to report the next morning when he started back to work.

Jake dragged in their stuff, considerably more since he'd emptied the garage apartment and loaded the rental truck for their return.

"Get used to it, buddy," he muttered as he looked around the crowded room. "No more nomad life for you."

After he'd stacked the items in the house, he went to turn in the truck. At the truck rental place, he unhooked his car from the tow bar, took the car seat from the cab of the truck, and returned it to the backseat of his car.

"You ready to go see Laurie?" he asked Teddy as he settled his son in the car.

"See Laurie?" The child looked excited.

Jake smiled at his son's question. "Come on, buddy. Time to work on getting me a wife and you a mom."

Suzanne had invited them to dinner when he called earlier to tell her when they would arrive. Greg was parking in the driveway and they walked into the house together, Jake's arms filled with Teddy and two bouquets of flowers.

"You trying to make me look bad to my woman?" Greg teased.

"Hostess gift."

Greg led the way through the house, Yapper welcoming them with her excited barks.

"Jake," Suzanne called. He managed a hug and handed her

one of the bouquets. He looked around. "Where's Laurie?"

"In her room." She reached for Teddy. "Why don't you go say hello?"

Lauren rested on the bed, her legs covered with her mother's memory quilt. It pleased him that Suzanne had shared her treasure in Laurie's time of need. Her earbuds were in place and her eyes closed. When she didn't respond, he sat on the side of the bed and leaned forward to kiss her cheek.

Her smile was all the reassurance he needed. Jake kissed her, his lips lingering as the impact of the connection filled him with confidence. "I'm home."

The hazel gaze fixed on him. "Where's Teddy?"

"With your mom. I brought you these."

She cradled the roses in her casted arms. "They're beautiful. Thank you."

"How are you feeling?"

"Okay. They replaced the casts yesterday, and the doctor says I'm healing well."

"Good. I'm going to need your help at the office."

"What made you change your mind?"

Lauren's eyes never left his face, and Jake considered his vow to give her time, but he needed to know if she cared for him. "There's this beautiful woman who haunts my dreams. I came back to see if she feels the same for me."

Her eyes widened. "You love me?" She put a casted hand over her mouth.

He grinned broadly. "I do. But I need to explain why I left."

He propped against the headboard, and she leaned against his chest. Jake wrapped his arms about her and felt a contentment he'd never experienced before. "I once said I'd never become involved with another needy woman."

Jake could see from her crestfallen expression that she'd misunderstood what he was trying to say. He explained about his marriage to Gwen.

"You're not needy," he corrected quickly. "Neither was Gwen. I was the selfish one. That same selfishness is why I held back even though I knew I cared for you. I told myself I couldn't give you what you need."

"You're afraid of my problem," Lauren whispered.

Jake tipped her face up and looked into her beautiful face. "Actually I'm more afraid I won't do the right things, but I promise to try. Mom suggested I pray over the matter, and I felt God leading me to come back. I won't blame you if you don't want to try," he said finally. "I understand completely."

Her features became more animated. "There are things in life that are as necessary as the air we breathe," Lauren told him. "There's no way I'd walk away from what we could have, though it won't be easy."

"It wouldn't be anyway," Jake said without doubt. "Your narcolepsy is one more thing we'll have to work our way around."

"I feel like the selfish one right now," she told him. "I know I should tell you to find someone else. But I can't let you go."

"I don't want to. We're going to take this slow, Laurie. I'm going to show that love I've been hiding from you and in time, I want to make you my wife. We'll work together in your company and raise Teddy. Happiness will be ours because God will direct our paths and answer our prayers and we will be content in our love."

She looked down at her hands, obviously frustrated by the casts. "You know these are your fault."

"Mine?"

"I was thinking about you and not paying attention to where I was going."

Jake hugged her closer. "What were you thinking?"

She shrugged. "About what you were doing. Wondering if you were happy. That kind of thing."

He smiled. "I'll gladly take the blame. But you have to

promise not to let it happen again. We can't spend our married life with your hands in casts because you were daydreaming."

Lauren's head moved from side to side. "Oh, never again. Next time I fall, I won't use my hands to stop my fall."

"Come on," he urged, swinging his feet off the bed. "You've got to see Teddy. He's growing so fast."

They went into the family room and found Teddy running after Yapper.

"Oh, Jake, he's gotten so big. Hey, buddy."

The child looked up and a beatific grin split his face as he raced headlong toward her. "Laurie, Teddy back."

Lauren fell to her knees and reached for him, beaming as she hugged him close.

Tears wet Jake's eyes, and he smiled sheepishly at Suzanne as he reached to wipe them away. She did the same as she mouthed a thank-you to him.

☙

One year later

Lauren glanced up when the back door opened and Jake stepped inside. She finished stirring the contents of the Crock-Pot that held their dinner and grinned up at him.

"There's my beauty." He piled his things on the table before tugging her into his arms for a hug and long kiss. "Missed you."

His words thrilled her as much as his touch. While she still suffered from attacks, Lauren knew God had healed her in a way she never imagined. He'd sent her someone to cherish, and she felt healed by Jake's wonderful love. "I was only gone for the afternoon."

He looped his arms about her waist and looked into her eyes. Gerry Hart had picked her up at the office and driven her to the doctor's office that afternoon. The woman continued to stay with Teddy and Yapper and help around the house. They had grown closer and just that afternoon in the doctor's office Gerry apologized to Lauren for the pain they had caused her all those years ago.

"You don't need to apologize. I understand."

"I don't," Gerry said. "There was no reason for us to be afraid. Melanie said the same thing when we talked at Thanksgiving. She said you didn't deserve it. I think she understands even more since her little girl was diagnosed with Down syndrome."

"I'm sorry." Lauren hugged her.

"How did the appointment go?" Jake's question pulled her back to the present.

"Good." She leaned away slightly and called, "Teddy, Daddy's home." She turned back to Jake. "He's been looking for you ever since we got home."

The two-year-old made his way into the kitchen doing double-time, his arms raised into the air. "Daddy."

Jake grinned and grabbed him up, swinging him about before giving him a big smack on the cheek. "Hey, buddy."

A flurry of words poured from the toddler's mouth, some understandable, others nearly unintelligible. He patted his chest and said, "See shirt."

Lauren grinned. She'd wondered if he would do what she'd taught him.

"You got a new shirt?" Jake asked, holding him out slightly so he could read the writing. "Lauren?" he began, his gaze widening when he read I'M GOING TO BE A BIG BROTHER.

She nodded. "It's going to be scary, Jake. I'll have to go off my medication until after the baby is born."

He jerked out a chair and urged her to sit. "Are you okay with this?"

"I'm happier than I ever dreamed possible. Mom and Dad will be over the moon."

"They don't know."

She grinned and shook her head. "Not before you. They'll be home from their trip this weekend. I thought we might have a special dinner."

"Sure. Whatever you want," he said.

"They never dreamed they would have grandchildren. Teddy is such a blessing to them." She touched her stomach. "And now this baby will add to their joy."

He set Teddy on his feet and dropped to his knees next to her. "And mine. I love you, Laurie."

Her arms went about his neck, her fingers smoothing his hair. "You've given me so much, Jake. Love I never dreamed I'd have in my life, my own home, a wonderful son in Teddy, and now this baby. I don't know how I ever lived without you. You're all those dreams I told you about rolled into one." She sniffed and giggled. "I think we finally found a reason to change this place."

He shook his head. "We can add on, but there's one thing this place has that will never change."

"The love?"

He nodded and held her tight.

They had fought past the fears of human nature and come out stronger for their efforts. Lauren prayed daily that their bond of love and faith would indeed be the mountain-moving kind.

Once she'd longed to touch the hem of Jesus' garment and be healed, but instead she'd been given the touch of this wonderful man who had made a difference in her life. His touch soothed, comforted, and conveyed caring in ways she'd never imagined possible, and because of his love, she'd learned to trust and reach out to others. Lauren knew without doubt that all along God had known Jake would be just what she needed.

A Letter To Our Readers

Dear Reader:

In order that we might better contribute to your reading enjoyment, we would appreciate your taking a few minutes to respond to the following questions. We welcome your comments and read each form and letter we receive. When completed, please return to the following:

Fiction Editor
Heartsong Presents
PO Box 719
Uhrichsville, Ohio 44683

1. Did you enjoy reading *Just One Touch* by Terry Fowler?
   ❏ Very much! I would like to see more books by this author!
   ❏ Moderately. I would have enjoyed it more if

   _____
   _____
   _____

2. Are you a member of **Heartsong Presents**? ❏ Yes ❏ No
   If no, where did you purchase this book? _____
   _____

3. How would you rate, on a scale from 1 (poor) to 5 (superior), the cover design? _____

4. On a scale from 1 (poor) to 10 (superior), please rate the following elements.

   ____ Heroine   ____ Plot
   ____ Hero   ____ Inspirational theme
   ____ Setting   ____ Secondary characters

5. These characters were special because? _____

_____

_____

6. How has this book inspired your life? _____

_____

_____

7. What settings would you like to see covered in future
   Heartsong Presents books? _____

_____

_____

8. What are some inspirational themes you would like to see
   treated in future books? _____

_____

_____

9. Would you be interested in reading other **Heartsong
   Presents** titles? ❑ Yes ❑ No

10. Please check your age range:
    ❑ Under 18   ❑ 18-24
    ❑ 25-34   ❑ 35-45
    ❑ 46-55   ❑ Over 55

Name _____

Occupation _____

Address _____

City, State, Zip _____

E-mail _____

Life is like the poster on the wall of the doctor's office—one of those inspirational quotes framed in misty pink flowers.

There are years that ask questions, and years that answer—Zora Neale Hurston.

It's not easy to be so profound when life actually starts asking questions you can't answer—not just one or two narrow questions, but a barrage of broad, complex, open-ended questions. A flood, my Grandma Rose would have called it. "Sometimes life goes by in a trickle, and sometimes life goes by in a flood," she used to say. "It's in those rainy seasons, you find out how well you can swim." When she said that, I had no idea what she meant. I never listened much to Grandma Rose. She had an old-fashioned, bible-thumping, show-me-state Baptist lecture on every subject, and she wasn't shy about dealing them out. I was busy, confident, on top of the world, a modern woman. I didn't have time to listen to what she was trying to tell me. My life was all about things I could program and control—microprocessors, and LAN networks, and wireless links that move at the speed of light.

I had no experience with realities that couldn't be controlled through data switches and efficiently written code. I knew nothing about surviving a flood because I'd never been in one. I was safely entrenched, or in a rut—it depended on how you looked at it. The problem with ruts is that when it starts to rain, they flood easily.

Things were, all-in-all, pretty good in my particular rut. Even with the trauma of September Eleventh, and the fact that my husband was an airline pilot, we were fairly content. I had a good career, he had a good career. We had sufficient income for what we wanted. We had friends, and activities, and, after a few years of living out in California, we were back in Boston, where I grew up and where we first met fourteen years ago on an incoming flight. We'd settled into a trendy converted loft in the old Leather District—*the* place to be, if you knew Boston well enough to get past the tourist hype. Sometimes, we both ended up there on the weekend. Together.

The day I read that quote from Zora Neale Hurston was the day everything changed.

I was staring at the misty floral poster in Dr. Conner's office when he told me that my second set of tests hadn't come back normal. I didn't hear him at first—I was thinking that I needed to get back to the Lansing building for the two o'clock management meeting about the newest round of layoffs. If Dr. Conner didn't hurry up, I'd be late. Why didn't doctors realize that everyone else's time was just as valuable as theirs?

"It could be cancer again, Karen," he said.

That one word sliced through my consciousness with the silent swish of an arrow, bisecting everything I was thinking. *Cancer. It could be cancer again, Karen.* My mind rushed back eight years to the first time a doctor said that to me. Back to the day I miscarried the tiny baby that was growing inside me, and the doctor, during the D & C that followed, seemed concerned about more than just the miscarriage. He said the same thing then, *It could be cancer.* And it was. A lab test confirmed it.

Surgery removed the spots, and a partial hysterectomy took away the chance of ever having children, but it couldn't remove the guilt. It was my own fault for convincing myself that, since James and I weren't at the point of planning any children, I could skip the dreaded annual visit to the gynecologist. Eventually, I'd skipped for so many years that I was afraid to go back. Even after I knew I was accidentally pregnant following our romantic seven-year anniversary trip to Fiji, I put off going to the doctor for a week, two, three, until ten weeks into the pregnancy, I started cramping and spotting, and I knew something was very wrong.

Now here we sat again, me with my stomach full of the old fear, and Dr. Conner looking at me in that regretful-but-businesslike way.

"Karen?" I realized he was talking to me.

"Wh . . . what?" I heard myself say. All I could do was stare at the pink poster on the wall.

"Don't start worrying yet. The biopsy is just a precaution, because the lab detected some inflamed cells on your slide. Seventy-five percent of uterine cancer reoccurrences occur within the first three years, and you've been cancer-free for eight years now. Odds are the tissue sample will come back negative, but we need to go ahead with the biopsy, just to be certain."

"Today?" I muttered. *I have to go to a management meeting. The company's doing a new round of layoffs today. I have to be there to tell my people . . .*

"No, not today, but let's schedule it soon."

"Sure," I said, standing up and reaching for my purse in the chair, feeling my fingers close numbly over the handle. "I'll schedule it on my way out."

Dr. Conner patted my shoulder again, ushering me through the door. "Good. No point spending time wondering and worrying. Let's just do the test, and that'll put the question behind us."

There are years that ask questions. Years . . . "All right." I started down the hall, and I could feel Dr. Conner watching me. Slowing as I came near the reception desk, I watched the doctor slip into another exam room. When he was gone, I kept walking, past the desk, through the waiting room door, past the pregnant ladies in the uncomfortable chairs, through the plate glass exit, across the marble lobby where my heels echoed against the silence, and onto the Boston street. I stood there gulping air, leaning against the cool exterior of the building, feeling like I wanted to kick my shoes off and run . . . somewhere.

National Bestselling Author
Lisa Wingate

Texas Cooking

No one is more surprised than Colleen Collins when she's offered a job writing a fluffy magazine article about rural Texas cooking. But after only a few days in the charming little town of San Saline, the big-city reporter is falling for the local residents, and finding it impossible to reisist the frustrating True McKitrick, a local-boy-made-good whose mere presence makes her feel alive—and at home.

0-451-41102-1

"WINGATE WRITES WITH DEPTH AND WARMTH; JOY AND WIT." —DEBBIE MACOMBER

"EVERYTHING ROMANCE SHOULD BE, YET SO MUCH MORE." —CATHERINE ANDERSON

Available wherever books are sold or at
www.penguin.com

O011

Stephanie Gertler

The Puzzle Bark Tree
0-451-20884-6

When Grace Hammond Barnett's parents die suddenly, she is bequeathed a lakeside house she never knew existed. Leaving her city life behind, she travels to the house for refuge and meets a man who helps her unravel a devastating secret buried in her past.

"ENGAGING...INSIGHTFUL CONTEMPORARY FICTION."
—*MIDWEST BOOK REVIEW*

Jimmy's Girl
0-451-20516-2

Do you ever think back on your first love? This acclaimed debut novel explores the "what if" questions that live in every woman's heart.

"A PERFECT REMINDER OF HOW STRONG FIRST LOVE CAN BE...DEFINITELY A PAGE-TURNER."
—*REDBOOK*

Available wherever books are sold or at
www.penguin.com

NA671

Nineteenth-century Ireland was a place of harsh suffering and haunting beauty, of famine and fortune. This is the novel of one extraordinary woman living through the darkest of times—and finding hope in the future.

Gracelin O'Malley

by Ann Moore

"A grand story."
—Eileen Goudge

"A beautiful book."
—Cathy Cash Spellman

"Historical fiction at its finest."
—Publishers Weekly

"Truly great fiction."
—Historical Novels Review

0-451-21241-X

Available wherever books are sold or at
www.penguin.com

A551